Orange Harvest

Orange Harvest

Third in the Orange Trilogy

by

Angela Fields

Also by Angela Fields
Orange Champagne
Sweet Orange

Chapter 1

January 23, 1968
North Korea seizes the USS Pueblo, claiming the surveillance ship strayed into its waters. One U.S. crewman is killed and 82 others are imprisoned; an 11-month standoff with the United States follows.

Mac MacKenzie's son got up from the sofa and turned off the television set. He was tired of watching the same news night after night. The number of troops who had been killed that day in Vietnam. The protests taking place on the college campuses throughout the country. Racial unrest. He was sick of it all. The country was in such a mess, so different than the one he grew up in. And to think that today's troops came home and got spit on! And many of them then went on to join the protesters. You never would have seen his fellow Marines doing something like that after WWII. It was unfathomable to him. And now this. U.S. sailors imprisoned by the damn commies.

Alex couldn't take any more of it. He went into the kitchen and made himself a sandwich and grabbed a beer, then went upstairs to his bedroom, where he lit the fire and sat on the settee in front of it. For the hundredth time, he told himself he needed to do something about redecorating the place. It still looked the way it did when he was a kid. His mother had attempted to redecorate after the war but didn't go too far other than to change the reds and oranges to pale blues and greens in the living room and bedroom. *Oh well, later*, he thought.

Tonight's event didn't appeal to him, but he knew he had to go. It was the grand opening of the MacKenzie Museum of Local History. This would be the first time he would be seeing it, even though he had wholly funded it. His father had told him when he was a kid to support the arts, and this was a way of doing that. He wasn't really interested in it. As a matter of fact, he wasn't much interested in anything these days. He didn't care about cars. He drove a 1960 Ford pickup. He didn't care about clothes. His daily uniform was Levis and a plaid shirt. He didn't care about having a close relationship with a woman. He had several women he saw intermittently, but they knew he wasn't looking for a commitment. And for the past couple of years there was Donna. She had been gone since November and, truth be told, he didn't really miss her. There was a woman who fascinated him, but she was off limits. He didn't care about movies. The last time he went to a movie theater was in 1962. That was when he went to see *The Man Who Shot Liberty Valance*. Now it was on tv.

Finishing the sandwich, he took the remainder of the beer into the bathroom. He needed to shower and dress for this affair.

Alex pulled into the parking lot, handed his keys to the valet, and approached the museum. He smiled as he walked past his father's 1922 Model D Packard truck, which was on display just outside the entrance to the museum. His dad loved Packards, getting a new car every couple of years. But he kept the work trucks longer, and this was the one he was still using when he died in 1930. The museum staff had done a nice job restoring it, and he was pleased. Walking into the lobby, he was impressed with what he saw. The building was beautiful. The wood was rustic, rough-sawn and splintered, giving it an old western feel. Incongruously, everything else in the place was elegant. There was a Georgia O'Keefe painting in the lobby, exhibited to maximum effect by the soft glow of the recessed lights above it. A large Frederick Remington sculpture of a cowboy on horseback was on display in the center of the lobby, on a raised pedestal. He knew that both pieces were reproductions. The woman who had been hired (not by him, but by the curator of the museum) sent him reports of her purchases. She was always asking for more money, reminding him that a museum couldn't only house reproductions, it needed original artwork. He supposed she was right and continued to provide funding for her purchases, but he couldn't justify buying originals when art wasn't the focus of the museum. He looked forward to seeing the museum beyond the lobby, but he had been told he needed to speak for a few minutes before the museum was opened for view. So for now he stood in the lobby drinking a Scotch from the open bar funded by himself.

Alexander wasn't uncomfortable in this setting. He could dress up and mingle with the best of them. He just didn't care for it. He'd rather be home reading a Louis L'Amour book for the third or fourth time. But he had put on his new Botany 500 suit, black and tailored to fit him perfectly. Although he was 48 years old, the work he did around the ranch kept him in good shape, and he knew the suit showed off his trim physique. When the time came, he'd step up to the podium and charm the ladies and gentlemen, and they'd never guess he would rather be home by himself.

Someone bumped into him from behind. "Oh, I'm so sorry, sir!" She stepped in front of him to face him. "Hello. I'm Rose Lefebre, art buyer for the museum." *My goodness but he's handsome*, she thought. He reminded her a little of Maximilian Schell, but with dimples.

"Nice to meet you, Rose. I take it you're responsible for the O'Keefe and the Remington here in the lobby. Nice choices." She was wearing what he had heard referred to as a "little black dress." It was sleeveless and short, above her knees. Her hair was pulled back into some kind of a knot. It was combed straight back, flattering her face and showing off her large brown eyes. Her eyelashes were excessively long and thick, probably false as was the current fashion, thanks to the British model, Twiggy. The British Invasion had dominated American culture, and it didn't stop with the music. Rose was holding a long cigarette holder in the same hand she was holding her champagne glass, giving her a very sophisticated air.

"Yes, but you know they're just reproductions. I would have died to get the originals!"

"These are nice the way they are. I like the way they're displayed."

"I would have much preferred the originals. But as it was, I had to beg for every penny I got. The funder is very tight with his money."

"Is that so?"

"Oh yes! I had to keep going back and begging him for more money. If he'd have given me a decent budget in the beginning, I wouldn't have had to grovel like I did."

"So you're saying he's a tightwad?"

"Ridiculously so."

"Can I get you another glass of champagne?"

As he was handing her the new glass of champagne, the mayor came up to him and told him it was time for him to say a few words. He left Rose standing there and followed the mayor up to the podium. The mayor introduced him as Alexander MacKenzie, benefactor of many establishments in the area, of which this museum was the latest. As Alex stood before the podium, he saw the back of Rose as she was exiting the lobby. It brought a smile to his handsome face, and he looked all the more charming as he began to speak.

After the speech, the gallery rooms were opened, and he moved from room to room enjoying himself more than he had expected to. The original horse-drawn plough that his father used to plant the first orange grove was there, as was his original branding iron. Other ranchers had contributed items too. They were all nicely displayed with plaques explaining their origins and use. Original artwork hung on the walls. These were done by local artists, most of whom were not known outside the area, and Alex had been happy to support the purchases. Even though the pieces weren't local "history," they leant a nice touch and gave the place some class.

The curator, Mr. Young, approached him. Rose was on his arm. "Mr. MacKenzie, I wanted to personally thank you for your generosity. I hope we've pleased you with our creation. I'd like to introduce our buyer, Miss Rose Lefebre."

"We've met," she responded tersely, and then turned her head as though she was looking for someone.

"I'll leave you two to discuss your purchases, Rose. I think you'll be very pleased to learn of her acquisitions, Mr. MacKenzie." He walked away and left Alex and Rose once again facing each other.

"You shouldn't smoke, you know," chastised Alex.

"That's really none of your business. Anyway, I don't. I just like the way it looks in this cigarette holder. Don't you agree?"

"Agree? That your pretense is attractive?"

Rose had never met anyone like him. He was arrogant. No, he was just plain rude. You'd think with all that money he would have at least learned some manners.

"You should have told me."

"Told you what?"

He was infuriating. "Told me who you were."

"Were? You mean 'am'"?

"Are you naturally this exasperating or do you work at it?"

"I'm just giving you a bad time. We tightwads are like that." This brought a smile to her face.

"I'm sorry I was so impudent. I'm actually very appreciative of everything you gave me. You never turned me down. It was just embarrassing to have to keep asking."

"You should have come by the house and told me in person that you needed more money up front. I didn't know! How about if I make it up to you?" He inwardly laughed that she had gotten him to apologize to her when she had been the one who made the faux pas.

"How would you do that?"

"Have you eaten?"

"No, I was so busy making sure everything was ready for the opening I didn't even think about eating." That didn't surprise him. She was a skinny little thing.

"What do you say we go get some food? I think this event is wrapping up anyway." They walked out and around to the parking lot, passing his father's locomotive. What an ordeal that had been to get it moved over to the museum! But this is where it belonged; he was sure his dad would agree. They gave the attendant their parking stubs. She would follow him in her own car. His truck was the first one to be brought up front, and she looked at him rather quizzically. His truck, an eight-year-old two-tone turquoise and white Ford, was a work truck that showed its age and utility in the dents and scratches it bore. Before he said anything, her car came up. A black convertible Porsche 911. He smiled at her and shook his head as he got into his truck.

She followed him in to Riverside, down University Ave. to D'Elia's Grinders. He pulled into a space in the parking lot and she pulled into one next to him. At 10:30 p.m. the place was crowded, and they weren't the only customers there who were dressed for an evening out. "I wasn't expecting this," she said.

"No? Best place around for pastrami sandwiches." He ordered one for each of them and two Cokes and ushered her to a table. "So, Miss Rose Lefebre, tell me about yourself."

She looked at him, somewhat intimidated by how handsome he was. "I grew up in Placentia. On an orange grove."

"Really? So we have something in common." Alex's father had planted 10,000 acres in orange groves. They were still thriving and made up much of his expansive ranch.

"Yes, we do. But my parents are selling off our land. They're tired of the business and the land is now more valuable for housing subdivisions than it is for growing oranges." Since the war ended in 1945, an unprecedented housing boom was created in Southern California. It seemed as though every serviceman who had ever come through its sunny ports had returned after the war to call the place home. As they created the baby boom generation, houses and schools couldn't be built fast enough. The price of land was at a premium to accommodate these new transplants.

"I know it is. I'm trying to decide what to do with my ranch. I feel like I'd be letting my dad down if I started selling it off. But you're right about it being more valuable for housing."

"Your father's ranch is legendary. But I suspect he knew well the value of a dollar. If he were here today he might sell if off himself."

"I've thought about that many times. Did your parents start your groves?"

"Oh no. My mother's grandmother did."

"What do you do when you're not buying artwork with someone else's money?"

She gave him an offended look. "My life is art. Did you know I'm a friend of Andy Warhol?"

"No, I didn't. You're proud of that?"

"Proud of it? Of course I'm proud of it! He's even considering me for one of his 15-minute films!"

"Wow. What would you be doing? Eating? Sleeping? Slurping tomato soup?"

"I don't know! And why do you make it sound so stupid? It's an honor!"

"If you say so. Are you done?" She had only taken a few bites of her sandwich, then hadn't touched it for the remainder of their conversation.

"Yes, I am. I think I'm going to leave now."

"Give me your phone number?"

"What? Mr. MacKenzie, we have nothing in common!"

"That must be the attraction. And we do. Orange groves?" Grudgingly, but also flattered, she wrote out her phone number on a napkin and left. He watched her from behind as she walked out the door.

Chapter 2

January 30, 1968

*North Vietnamese communists launch the **Tet Offensive**. The assault contradicts the Johnson administration's claims that the communist forces are weak and the U.S.- backed south is winning the war.*

A week had gone by since he had seen her. Alex wasn't sure why he had put off calling her. She was so different than any of his other women. For one thing, she was young. He estimated she was in her early 30s, but of course he wasn't sure. Another thing, she was, what? Liberal? A leftie? He didn't know that for sure, but she admired Andy Warhol. That told him a lot. Probably was a war protester too. Nevertheless, he couldn't stop thinking about her. He unfolded the napkin he had been keeping in his wallet and picked up the phone.

Rose had given up on him. For the first few days she jumped every time the phone rang, only to be disappointed that it wasn't him. She had bought an extra-long phone cord so she could even take the phone into the bathroom with her when she took a bath, so as not to miss his call. But as the days wore on, she gave up and tried to stay busy so she wouldn't dwell on it.

She attended a protest in Balboa Park. The City Council had proposed tearing down a historical building in the park, in preparation for Balboa's bicentennial the next year. Several cultural groups had joined hands to encircle the building for the afternoon in a show of unity and support for preserving the building. She had just gotten home and was walking in the door when the phone rang. Her stomach did a rollover. "Hello?"

"Hi. Is this Andy Warhol's model?"

"Oh, hi." She tried to act like she had forgotten he was going to call. "You just caught me walking in. I've been at a protest in Balboa Park." That should assure him that she wasn't sitting around waiting for his call.

"A protest? You shouldn't be anywhere around protesters. They get violent."

Rose laughed. "Not these protesters. They're artists, architects, historians, and other cultural groups.

The City Council wants to tear down a historical building, so we surrounded it, holding hands in protest."

"I still don't like the idea of you being around protesters."

"Mr. MacKenzie, I can make up my own mind about how and where to spend my time."

"Anyway, what were you doing way down there? That's a long way from Riverside."

"I live in Laguna Beach."

"Ahhh, of course. The artists' colony." Since she didn't comment, he went on. "I was wondering if you'd like to get together and do something."

"What did you have in mind?

God, he hated this! He felt like he was back in high school. "You could come out to the ranch and I could show you around." He wished he had thought this through before he picked up the phone.

"I don't think so."

This was awkward and going nowhere fast. Then she offered, "Why don't you come down here and we can have lunch?" *Oh bless you*, he thought!

"Sure. I'd like that."

"I can also show you one of my paintings that's hanging in a local gallery."

"I'd really like that. When would you like to do that?"

"Not for a few days." She didn't really have anything to do, but she didn't want to appear over-anxious. "I'm going up to see my parents for a few days. My mother wants me to go shopping with her."

So she'd rather go shopping with her mother than spend time with him. "When do you think you'd like to get together?"

"Let's make it next Wednesday. I don't want to rush my mom."

"No, no of course not. OK, next Wednesday it is. I'll need an address and directions." She gave him the information and they hung up.

Screw her, he thought. He might not even go.

He got in his truck and drove out to the corral. He had started acquiring some of the wild mustangs the Bureau of Land Management had approved for adoption. Most of them came from Wyoming. It was a thrill for him to go up there and chase the horses, rope them, and bring them back to the ranch to be domesticated. Once home, the broncos had to be broken to a saddle. He had broken a few of them himself, but he found that he could barely walk the next day. Sprained back, sore neck, you name it. It was a job better left to the younger cowboys.

Their last roping in Wyoming was a month ago and had yielded a dozen horses. They had allowed time for the horses to get acclimated to their new environment and were just now beginning the process of breaking them. They were beautiful animals, and he knew they would sell for a lot. He climbed up and sat on the top rail of the fence and watched a cowboy bucking and breaking. Another cowboy approached him. "What's up, boss? Need something?"

"Nah, I just came out to watch. Beautiful animals, aren't they?"

"Oh yeah, sure are."

He stayed out there for about an hour, then drove over to the orange groves. He sat in his truck and watched the laborers work. His father had lain railroad tracks in and around his vast ranch. At the time, it was an efficient way to transport the oranges directly to market. He could hitch up the rail cars, laden with oranges, to a train headed for Los Angeles, or anywhere for that matter, and on to market. But transportation was much improved since his father's day. It became more cost efficient to load the produce onto semis, which didn't rely on train tracks to get to their destination. The tracks were still on the property and the locomotive had been moved to the museum.

So many of his father's accomplishments had changed since his death. Alex tried to honor his father by keeping up the ranch, but the older he got the more of a burden it became to him. He had once heard someone use the term albatross to describe a burden. It dawned on him that that is what this ranch was, an albatross. A burden that feels like a curse. Thinking about it made him feel ashamed, so he put the thought out of his mind.

Alex went home, showered, and sat on the sofa downstairs pondering what might be done with the house. It needed work. And not just the décor. It needed to be rewired, replumbed, re-everythinged. He was reminded of this every time he sat in the living room. It was faded and long out of date. Besides that, his mother's taste tended toward the bland. He knew it could look a lot better. He just didn't know how to do it.

Chapter 3

February 7
After a battle for the Vietnamese village of Ben Tre, an American officer tells Associate Press reporter Peter Arnett, "It became necessary to destroy the town in order to save it." The quotation, printed in newspapers nationwide, becomes a catchphrase for the opponents of The Vietnam War.

He left his house about 11:00 to get to Laguna by noon. Now that the 91 Freeway was completed, it would only take him about an hour. The drive took him from Riverside County into Orange County, named for the industry that put it on the map. As he neared Laguna Beach, he could smell the ocean air. It was nice and he breathed in a large measure of it.

Following the directions Rose had given him he had no trouble finding her house. It was on a cliff overlooking the ocean. The house was made of redwood, a wood that held up to the coastal elements.

Through the years, the redwood had faded, now giving it the appearance of driftwood. Hanging plants in macramé hangers hung from the rafters above the porch. Ceramic sculptures sat below them. Beachy, he thought. And artsy. He rang the bell.

Rose answered, wearing black capris pants and a long, loose sweater. In Southern California February was usually sunny and mildly crisp. Once again, her hair was in a knot at the back of her head. She was barefoot. "You made it. Please come in."

The inside of her house looked a lot like the outside. Lots of plants, statuary, wall hangings in various media, including one that looked like it was macraméd from colored rags. Two beanbag chairs had been haphazardly tossed next to a low sectional. It was different than the houses he was used to visiting. "Can I get you something to drink?"

"Is it too early for a Scotch?"

She laughed, and as she disappeared into the kitchen she turned her head and said, "Have a seat." He wasn't sure where to sit. Certainly not on a beanbag. He lowered himself onto the very low sofa. Rose returned with a Scotch on ice. "Hope you wanted ice in it." Usually he had it neat, but he just said, "Thank you." She positioned herself on the other end of the sectional, which made it easy for them to have eye contact while keeping their distance.

A pretty little Calico cat came sauntering in to meet the guest. "That's CaliCat," Rose informed him.

As Alex bent down to pet it, Rose warned, "Be careful, she doesn't act nearly as pretty as she looks." Just as she said that CaliCat turned and clawed his arm, leaving deep scratches.

"Ouch! So how long have you lived here?"

"Ever since I got out of college, which was 10 years ago." He had guessed her age about right.

"Nice view," he responded.

"I'm fortunate. I'm not your typical starving artist. My family is wealthy."

"Something else we have in common," and he lifted his glass as in a toast. "Orange groves were the thing in the last century. We owe it to our ancestors for their foresight."

"Yes, my great-grandparents and your…father? How could that be? He couldn't have been old enough to develop a ranch that size in the last century."

"Oh, he was. He was almost 70 when I was born. I was 10 when he died in '30." Rose did a quick calculation. That meant he was 48 years old. *Too old*, she wondered? "And the ranch isn't just oranges. We've got cattle too. And in the past few years I've started selling mustangs."

"Cars? Do you own a dealership?"

This brought him a genuine laugh. "No, honey. Wild horses." Now it was her turn to laugh. She was embarrassed. She felt like a silly young girl asking such a stupid question.

"Would you like to see the rest of the house?" She needed to change the subject, and quickly. She showed him the kitchen, which was nice but small. There were herbs and other things sprouting in a variety of ceramic vases and bowls, probably all hand made by her or her friends, he surmised. There were ferns everywhere, placed on tables and hanging from the ceiling. There was a large spider plant with about 20 baby "spiders" hanging off the main plant. He also noticed she had a collection of African violets. The first of the two bedrooms looked just like the rest of the house, beachy and rather bohemian. When she opened the door into her own bedroom, she leapt up onto the bed and rolled about as though she were on sailboat in stormy seas.

"Not a waterbed!" he proclaimed, somewhat in shock. This girl really was too young for him. Why was he so attracted to her?

"Yes! It's absolutely groovy! C'mon. Give it a try!"

"Uh, no. Not right now." He had never been on a waterbed and certainly wasn't about to get on one now.

"Oh, silly. OK, let me show you my yard." The backyard was small. Tall Cyprus and eucalyptus trees blocked out any view from the neighbors, giving it complete privacy. "Maybe we can go in the hot tub later."

Oh my God, she's a hippy. The rest of the yard was overgrown in plants: herbs in large pots, lavender bushes, succulents in pots hanging from the eaves. He didn't look too closely for fear he'd find marijuana plants growing in among the other foliage.

"And over here, you see this deck? It's my meditation deck. It's also where I do my yoga."

This is never going to work out. "What do you say we go get that lunch?"

They drove downhill and found an outdoor café. The weather was mild, but still cool, so they found a place to sit in the sun. They both ordered fish and chips with a green salad to start. She had a Coke and he had water.

"So tell me about this painting of yours we're going to see."

"You remembered! So I work in what they call abstract expressionism. Are you familiar with it?"

"No, I can't say I am."

"It grew out of surrealism and it's primarily an American movement. It's so popular that many believe New York is surpassing Paris as the leader of modern art."

"Wow."

"Some of the names associated with it are Jackson Pollack, Roy Lichtenstein, William de Koonig, of course, he's Dutch, also Mark Rothco, oh, and so many others." Alex had heard of Jackson Pollack. He thought he might be the one who splattered paint on large surfaces.

"But I'm mostly inspired by the women in the movement." *A feminist, I should have figured.* Rose continued, "Of course Helen Frankenthaler, everyone knows her, but also Ethel Schwabacker, Sonia Getchtoff, Perle Fine, and so many others. I'm really flattered that you want to see my work!" Alex had never heard of any of these people.

They finished their lunch and drove to the gallery. It was small, but apparently popular as there were about a dozen other people viewing the artwork displayed on the walls and on tables. There was a life-size sculpture in the center of the gallery that depicted Christ, nude, with a crown of thorns on his head and holding an M2 carbine rifle, one of the main weapons currently being used in Vietnam. Alex hadn't been to church since he was a kid, but right now he felt like he needed to go to confession. "Do you like this?" he asked, gesturing toward the sculpture.

"It makes a statement."

"Do you agree with the statement?"

"I hate the fact that young men are dying in a war that no one understands. But no, I really don't like to see Christ's image used like that." *OK, that's not too bad*, he thought.

She led him to a far wall and pointed out her painting. Stepping back, with her arm outstretched as though announcing "tah-dah," she reminded him of a proud kindergartner showing off her first finger painting. And that's pretty much what it looked like. Turquoise finger painting. "Well, what do you think?" she prompted.

"It's uh, nice! Interesting! Is it making a statement?"

"Abstract expressionism is an art born out of the expression of the self, of profound emotions. In this, I'm depicting the universal theme of conflict vs. beauty. Do you like it?" *Is conflict the opposite of beauty?* he mused.

"Yes! I think it's, uh, very creative. You've got quite a talent there, Miss Rose Lefebre. Is it for sale?"

"Yes, but it's only been on display for about a month. The gallery owner wanted to list it for $295, but I suggested we wait and see what somebody offers. So far no one has made an offer."

"I'm sure someone will. It's a beautiful piece of art." They ambled along the streets of Laguna, stopping in at several different galleries, Rose explaining the "statements" some of the paintings were making. In one shop he bought a hand-crafted ceramic pot in which Rose could plant some of her herbs.

As the afternoon light began fading, Alex suggested it was time he got back to the ranch. He walked her to the door, thanked her for the nice afternoon, and left.

Chapter 4

February 8, 1968

At the South Carolina State campus, police open fire on students protesting segregation at Orangeburg's only bowling alley. Three protesters die and 27 more are wounded. Nine officers are tried and acquitted of charges related to the use of force. A protest coordinator is convicted of inciting to riot, serves seven months in prison—and is pardoned 25 years later.

Rose awoke about 7:00 A.M. and immediately picked up her thoughts where they had left off when she fell asleep. Yesterday had been a nice day. She enjoyed herself with Alex, but she didn't think he had enjoyed his visit with her. He made her feel stupid. Young and stupid. He was, after all, 16 years her senior, practically old enough to be her father. And his life experience had been so different than hers. He had lost his father when he was a young boy. He had fought in the Pacific during the war, which meant he had seen carnage, lost friends, and killed enemy soldiers. She couldn't imagine what that must have been like. He came home and took over the family ranch, working hard to maintain what his father had established.

Her life had been carefree. She'd been raised in a grand house in the middle of the orange groves, her mother and older brothers spoiling her rotten. She went to school and studied art and art history, going to parties and doing pretty much anything she wanted to do. When she graduated, her parents bought her a house in Laguna Beach. It cost them a fortune, but they wanted her to be happy nestled in among other art-minded people. She had never had to do anything for anyone. Her role in life was to make herself happy. And she thought she was, that is, until now. All last night she questioned her value in the world, and those questions persisted this morning. It was because of him. She saw herself through his eyes, and she didn't particularly like what she saw. A shallow, self-centered young bohemian. No one to be taken seriously. And she thought she was part of the abstract expressionist movement? What deep, profound thoughts had she ever had? Alex thought she was a ninny and he was right.

It dawned on her that she really didn't know much about him. *And why was that?* she wondered. *Because I spent the whole day talking about myself. That's why.*

Alex had been up since 4:00 A.M. He had had trouble sleeping, his thoughts returning to the sprite he had spent the previous day with. She was too young for him. She had not experienced life. But was that fair to say? It wasn't her fault she was born too late and the wrong gender to fight in the war. She was only 9 years old when the war ended. She probably didn't even remember it. All she seemed to care about was art. Art that didn't include any pictures, looked like scribbles, but that apparently made a statement. What in the world would she know about conflict vs. beauty? What did that even mean, anyway? He had gotten a kick out of her. If he had to be honest, it was more than getting a kick out of her. He was falling for her. She made him feel young again. At the same time, she made him feel old.

But he knew she wasn't falling for him. She was like a butterfly, flitting from one thing to another, full of life and fun. He was old, disinterested in just about everything, and didn't even speak her language. She called the waterbed "groovy." No, he'd have to put her out of his mind and move on. Just like the other woman he had been trying to put out of his mind for the past two decades.

Alex's mother died in 1951. A couple of years later he decided to move into his parents' bedroom. After all, he was the master of the house now. He had called his Aunt Maddie to help him go through his mom's closet. The closet was the size of a small bedroom. As a matter of fact, at the other end of the hall was an identical space that actually was a bedroom. His father had opened up a doorway between the big bedroom and the smaller one, and outfitted the smaller one with hanging rods, shelves, and a large island in the middle with drawers beneath it and a ceramic surface for the top. He had done it for his first wife.

He had never talked to his father about the fact that he had been married before. He just always knew it. But shortly after his dad died, Aunt Maddie had made a comment about her grandmother, who was the first wife. Until then Alex had never made the connection between Maddie and this unknown woman.

Aunt Maddie was his favorite relative. When he was young, she could always be counted on to break a few rules in order to maximize their fun when she took him out. His half-sister, Laura, that is his mother's oldest child who was old enough to be his own mother, despised Maddie. She was always making comments about her wayward ways, her lack of values, and that she idolized money, which to her was blasphemy. Alex never thought any of that was true. She was just a fun person who could always be counted on for a good time. Now, nearing 70, she was married to an extremely rich plastic surgeon and lived in a mansion in the Hollywood

Hills.   Laura lived in a two-bedroom bungalow and continued to give her life and money to the Church of the Salvation of Sinners.

When Maddie had come down to help him clean out his mother's belongings, which also included many of his father's things, they discovered stacks of journals in the corner of the closet.   There was also a stack of framed sketches, apparently of the first wife.   His father had made them.   They were lewd, if not pornographic, many showing her in the throes of sexual pleasure.   They were also beautiful.   Alex spent the next several weeks reading the journals, which the first wife had written. From the journals, he could put the sketches in the order in which they'd been made.   When he was finished, he was fascinated if not in love with Dede O'Brien MacKenzie.

He knew that was crazy.   For one thing, she was long dead.   For another thing, she had been his father's wife.   Still in all, he couldn't get her out of his mind. What a woman! Beautiful, sexy, smart, kind, confident. And so accomplished!   Several times throughout the years, Alex wondered why his father had married his mother.   She was nothing like Dede.   Maybe, knowing he could never find another woman like Dede, he simply decided to find a nice woman with whom to share the remainder of his life.   Thinking about the comparison made him sad.   He was certain that his father had loved his mother; he was also certain that his father had been IN LOVE with Dede.   And now he was too.

In the ensuing years he had read Dede's journals several times. She had overcome so many hardships, the type most women would never know, thankfully. He got angry reading about the men who assaulted her, and about that jerk of a husband, Cole. In the beginning, he thought about her day and night. His obsession with her had waned through the years, but he still judged every woman he met against her.

Chapter 5

February 27
Walter Cronkite, in a CBS-TV special on his recent tour of Vietnam, says the U.S. war effort is "mired in stalemate" and amplifies public skepticism of the war.

It had been over two weeks since Alex had contacted Rose. He didn't know why he hadn't ever picked up the phone and called her. He certainly thought about her a lot. Now he wondered if he'd let too much time go by. Would she even remember him? Somewhat jealous, he wondered if she might have taken up with someone new. Someone more her age, someone better suited to her. He decided it was now or never and picked up the phone.

"Hello?"

"Did you get the herbs planted in your new pot?"

"Oh hi. I had given up on you. Yes, I planted thyme in the new bowl. It has a lot of health benefits, you know."

"I do now."

"Look, uh, Alex, I know we're really different, and I, uh, well, I, uh…"

"You'd rather I didn't call anymore? I understand."

"No! No, that's not what I was going to say. Uh, this is hard. Maybe we could meet for a drink and it would be easier for me to explain. Would you be ok with that?"

"Sure, I guess. What did you have in mind?

"Well, you could come down here again. There are a lot of little places where we could sit and talk."

Alex wasn't keen on the idea of driving all the way to Laguna just to listen to her say she didn't want to see him anymore. But he couldn't very well ask her to do the driving. "OK. This afternoon? I could be there about 4:00.

She wasn't expecting that, and it took her aback. But her reply was cool. "This afternoon would be fine. I'll see you then."

On his drive down there, he resolved to be more patient with her. He knew he had offended her a couple of times. He wanted to get to know her better, and he smiled thinking about that. When she would say they weren't right for each other, he'd have a promising comeback for her. He didn't know what that would be, but he'd come up with something.

He rang the doorbell at precisely 4:00. She opened it, and the first thing he noticed, couldn't help but notice, was that she had flowers in her hair. Her hair was down, and he was pleasantly surprised to see that it was long, almost down to her waist. But flowers? *She's a flower child. Why am I not surprised?* She was wearing a long, white, gauze skirt that gave her an ethereal look. She had on a gauze peasant top that fell off her shoulders. It had embroidery around the sleeves and he briefly wondered if she had done that handiwork herself. She was barefoot.

"Come in, Mr. MacKenzie. You're certainly punctual."

"When someone says 4:00, I believe you should arrive at 4:00."

CaliCat came in to see what was going on, and Alex moved to the other side of the room.

"I have something very exciting to tell you! But I want to wait until we're sitting down." Rose was glowing.

They got in his truck and she directed him to a small cantina on the sand. They found a table for two and the waiter brought out menus. He also brought chips in a woven plastic basket with wax paper in it. The accompanying salsa was served in a small bowl. "Something to drink?" the waiter asked.

Rose answered, "I'd like a margarita with a lot of salt on the rim."

He turned to Alex who told him to bring a cerveza. "Corona ok?" checked the waiter.

"That'd be fine." Turning to Rose, he asked, "So what's the exciting news?"

"My painting sold!"

"No kidding? Rose, that's great! You're a talented artist. You deserve to be recognized."

"And you'll never guess how much they paid for it! $1500! Can you believe it?"

"Yes, I can. A painting that depicts conflict vs. beauty is worth its weight in gold. I'm proud of you, Rose."

"You are?"

"Yes, I am." The waiter returned with their drinks and asked to take their order. "Did you want to have dinner?" Alex asked Rose. She ordered a shrimp burrito. He ordered a combo platter with two tacos and an enchilada.

"So, what did you want to talk to me about?" He braced himself. He still hadn't thought of a catchy comeback that would make her rethink her position.

She looked right at him. "We're very different."

"Yes, we are."

"I mean, you're practically old enough to be my father."

"I would have to have had you when I was in high school. That's a pretty young father." That elicited a chuckle from her.

"True. But you're kind of like in a different generation. You were in the war, like my brothers."

"Oh yeah? Where were they?"

"Charlie was in Italy. John was at the Battle of the Bulge."

"Good for them. Did they come out of it ok?"

"Oh yes. My oldest brother is an attorney and the other one is a high school principal."

"Both successful. So they're a lot older than you."

"Yes. Anyway, it just seems like you've had so much more life experience than I've had. I feel, uh, shallow next to you."

He winked at her. "I think you're charming."

"Charming? I behaved liked a silly ninny the last time you were here. I was certain that you'd never want to see me again."

Their food was delivered so they quit talking and each of them had their first bite. Then he continued.

"You're right. We are different. In age, in interests, in just about everything." Then, "I wonder why I can't get you out of my mind?" He smiled as he said this.

Rose was stunned, but she was determined to be cool. "I think about you a lot too."

"I'm still not clear on your position, Rose."

"Maybe I'm not either. And there's another thing. Everyone in my family has gone to college. I mean, I think I could be happy dating someone who hasn't, but I'm not sure what my family would think." Now it was his turn to be taken aback. She added, "I just want to be honest. I want to lay it all out on the table." Alex took his hand and rubbed his face, his eyes, cheeks, neck.

"I'm too old. I'm from a different generation. And you've been to college. Anything else? How about politics and religion. I'm a Republican and a Catholic, although I don't go to church."

"My parents and brothers are Republicans. I'm registered as an Independent. I really like Eugene McCarthy."

"Eugene McCarthy? You've gotta be kidding."

"But I am a Catholic! Bingo! We have something in common!"

"Would you like to continue to see me or not, Rose?"

"Well, I'd like to give it a try." With that they each rose their glasses in a mock toast and finished their dinner. Rose only ate about a fourth of her burrito.

By the time they left the cantina it was after 6:00. Rose told him that some of her friends were having a get-together and suggested that they stop in for a while. Alex agreed.

It was an apartment, and not a very nice one. The front door was open and as they approached Alex could smell the foul stench of marijuana. "Are you sure you want to do this, Rose?"

"Sure. These are my friends. Artists, Alex?"

They stepped in to find a group of about a dozen people sitting in a circle on the floor. Most of the young men had long hair and were barefoot. From a record player somewhere, Iron Butterfly was agonizing *In A Gadda Da Vida*. The air was thick with smoke. Rose introduced him to the people she knew, and then took a place around the circle. Alex sat on a metal chair at a thrift-shop dinette set. No one said much of anything, so Alex initiated the conversation.

"Any of you young men been in the military?"

A couple of the men guffawed. One of them coughed out, "Murderous pigs. They oughta all be shot with their own weapons." This brought some laughter from among the group.

"Really? They're over there saving your asses and you think they all need to be shot?"

"Hey dude, chill. They're over their killing women and children, burning entire villages. What gives them the right to determine who's right and who's wrong? Hell, even Walter Cronkite just came out against the war." He turned to his friends for confirmation. "Did you see that on the news today?" Some in the group nodded their heads.

"They're fighting a war against communism. The commies take over South Vietnam, who's to say what they'll take over next?" Alex wasn't actually sure how he felt about the war in Vietnam. He had a hard time making the connection to American citizens. His father had written him a letter before he died, which his mother had given him when he turned 18. In it, his father had admonished him not to fight other people's war. It had been different in WWII. America had been attacked. He was certain that his father would have approved of him joining up. After all, his dad had been a captain in the Army. But even with his questioning, America had decided it needed to fight the commies in far-off Southeast Asia, and that's what young men needed to do. He was disgusted with these pot-smoking losers.

Just then, the joint that had been making its way around the circle was handed to Rose. She took it, looked up at him in defiance, and took a long toke. He stood up and said, "I'm leaving. You coming with me, Rose, or are you going to find your own way home?"

Coughing, she answered, "I'll come with you."

As they got into the truck, he demanded, "What the hell were you doing?"

"It's just marijuana."

"Just marijuana. It's an illegal drug, Rose!

"You don't have to yell at me like I'm a child! And it's no worse than drinking alcohol."

"It's for degenerates! And it's illegal. You're acting like a child. Someone has to tell you what's right and what's wrong. Decent people don't sit around smoking marijuana!" She sat there, a tear streaming down her cheek. "And everyone's mouth had been on that thing. How do you know what they've got? Herpes, TB, who knows what?" She didn't speak, but the one tear had turned into many. He handed her a handkerchief. "You're too good for that, Rose. You're too good for that."

When they got back to her place, she opened the door and got out. She said, "Please don't get out. I'll be fine." He sat there until he saw she was inside the door safely.

He had only been home for about 10 minutes when the phone rang. When he answered it, she said, "I'm sorry."

"It's ok, Rose. We have some things we'll need to work out. We'll be ok."

"Really? You don't hate me?"

"No, not at all. You know, I was thinking that maybe you could come up to the ranch and give me some advice about redecorating my house."

He could hear her sniffling. She must have been crying the whole time he was driving home. "You want to redecorate your house?"

"I have to. I think the last time anyone did anything to it was right after the war. It needs a lot of help."

"Really?"

"Yeah, what do you say? Will you come up and give me some advice?"

"OK, if you're serious. When would you like me to come?"

"How about day after tomorrow? It's Thursday, and you can spend the whole weekend here. That is, if you want to. You can have your own guest room."

Chapter 6

February 29
The report of the Kerner Commission, appointed by President Lyndon B. Johnson to examine the causes of race riots in American cities in previous years, declares the nation is "...moving toward two societies, one black, one white – separate and unequal."

Heidi and Chloe, the two young women who meticulously cared for the house, were thrilled when Alex told him of his plans. Many times, out of earshot of Alex, they had complained to each other about how the house looked. They both thought that all the cleaning and fussing they did was lost in the faded, drab décor. They worked together to prepare a guest room for the woman who was coming to finally bring the house into the 20th century.

Rose was awestruck as she drove up the long driveway and got her first view of the house. Like everyone in Southern California, she had heard of the MacKenzie Ranch, but she always thought of farmland and cattle grazing. She had never stopped to consider that there was also a house on it. And if she had, she never would have envisioned one that looked like this. It was huge. There was a porch that ran the full width of the house and continued around each side, with six electric fans hanging from the roof of the front porch. Six wide steps led from the ground up to the porch and entryway. The front of the entire second floor was glass, and a deck wound its way from front to back. She wasn't sure what the house was made from, but she thought it might be cedar. It looked like a huge log cabin, but it wasn't made of round logs; it was made of flat planks.

A man, apparently anticipating her arrival, came out of the house and greeted her. "Hi, I'm Lee. Let me help you with your bag. Love your car!" Lee was Alex's best friend. Now both professed bachelors, they had been to high school together and had joined the Marines together. Lee had been awarded a Purple Heart for action on Guadalcanal. Rose noticed he walked with a limp.

"Oh, thanks. I'm Rose."

"Right in here, Rose. Alex should be down soon."

She was equally in awe of the size of the interior, which of course was equal in size to the exterior. A large fireplace was to her right, along the south wall. There was a sofa and two chairs in front of it. Above it was an impressionist reproduction that resembled a Monet, although it must not have been one of his because she wasn't familiar with it. Near the front window was another sitting area with a small couch and two more chairs. Along the far wall, in the corner, was a beautiful grand piano. Looking to her left, she saw a dining table and enough chairs for 12 people. The kitchen was beyond that. Despite its awesome size, the room was dull. *This place could be so beautiful*, she mused.

Just as she was considering what might be done to update the room, Alex descended the staircase. He was dressed in Levis and a plaid flannel shirt, the first she had ever seen him so casual. She liked it, and as she was when she first met him, was awestruck by how handsome he was.

"How was the drive?"

"Nice. I beat the rain."

"Yeah, it should be starting soon. You want something to drink? Actually, I thought you might be hungry so I had Heidi and Chloe fix something. Heidi? Chloe? Come out and meet Rose."

Introductions were made, then the two young women returned to the kitchen and brought out the lunch plates. On each plate was a small green salad, two crab cakes, and a sliced apple. They also brought out a platter of cheese and crackers. A pitcher of water was set on the table. Alex asked Rose if she'd rather have wine or something else. They both stuck with water.

"Alex, I had no idea your house was so huge!"

Chuckling, Alex said, "I think my dad got a little carried away. It's more like a hotel. Actually, that's pretty much what it was. Back in the day, when he'd have a dinner or some event, people would come from a distance and they'd need to stay overnight. So he built a place that could accommodate them."

"My goodness. How many rooms does it have?"

"There are four rooms running east and west on both sides of the lower level, so that's eight. The upper level has the same thing, so that's sixteen. Then, there's a large guest room at the top of the landing," he pointed to the top of the staircase, "that's where you'll be staying. And then there's the big bedroom which was my parents' room. I'm in there now. There's a small room on the south side of the landing, and a matching one next to the master bedroom, but my dad turned it into a closet."

"The whole bedroom? A closet?"

"Well, it was kind of small room, but yes. I'll show it to you later. It's a woman's dream closet, but right now I'm just storing some of my things in it."

"Wow! What do you do with all those rooms now?"

"They're all closed up and the furniture has dust cloths on it. Except for the room you're staying in. The girls keep that ready for guests."

"What are these two rooms down here, the ones right over there?" She pointed toward the east wall.

"The one on the left is my office. The one on the right was my mom's. She used it for doing her correspondence, and there's a sewing machine in there."

"Are you going to give me a grand tour?"

They started in the kitchen. It too was huge, but the appliances were old, as were the curtains, the paint, and everything else. She loved the huge worktable with a marble top sitting in the center of the room. She envisioned herbs hanging above it, right there ready to be picked and used as garnish in some gourmet dish.

Next, he opened the door to his mother's old work room, which held nothing of interest to Rose, except maybe the vintage sewing machine. Like the one next to it, this room had a set of French doors leading into it, but the glass was covered by shirred curtains so one really couldn't see into it.

He closed those doors and opened the doors to his office. As soon as she stepped in, her jaw dropped. "Like it? I thought you would."

"I'm speechless," she uttered as her eyes stared at the large turquoise painting hanging on the wall across from the doorway. When she looked up at him, he saw her eyes brimming with tears. "Why did you do that?"

"I'm still trying to figure it out. Just love abstract expressionism, I guess," he said with a wink.

"You must have thought I was so stupid, carrying on and on about how much someone paid for it, as though someone really thought my work was worth it. I shamelessly thought someone did."

"Someone did. But maybe not for the reasons you'd like to believe. Does it matter? Conflict vs. Beauty has found a place in someone's home, and it makes him smile every time he looks at it."

She cast her eyes downward. "Thank you." She looked up to see what else was in the room. She saw a diploma hanging on the left wall, above his desk. Princeton University. "Did your father go to Princeton?"

"No."

"Who, then?" she asked as she walked toward it. "Oh my. Aren't I just the biggest boor in the world?" Looking at him, she offered, "I'm so sorry, Alex. I had no idea."

"And you didn't think to inquire. You were so eager to assume that a lowly ranch hand couldn't be worthy of a woman with an art degree. Maybe now that you know your ranch hand has an MBA you'll reconsider."

"From Princeton, no less. Oh Alex. You must hate me."

"I should, shouldn't I?" They both chuckled. "But I don't. Just the opposite. I'm very attracted to you, Rose." He pulled her in close to him and held her. Her body stirred. After a minute, he kissed her forehead and released her. "Want to see the rest of the house?"

He escorted her up the stairs and opened the door to her room. Her eyes lit up. The room, like everything else in the house, was huge. A large bed sat in the middle of the room, its upholstered headboard against the north wall. There was a large vase of fresh flowers on a round table near the window, two bistro chairs with upholstered seats on either side of it. She walked over to the window and looked out on a large courtyard of perfectly manicured green grass. She saw a pool at the far end of the downward slope of the lawn. "You have a swimming pool?"

"Yes, but it's so old. I'm thinking about filling it in and having a new one installed up closer to the house."

The bedroom had no closet. Instead, it had a large wardrobe in which to hang one's suits or dresses, and a long dresser for folded clothing items.

With wide eyes, she looked at Alex. "And in here is your bathroom," he said. She stepped into the large bathroom, which had a black marble floor. A large claw-foot tub sat against one wall. There was an array of soaps and oils on a long thin shelf above the tub. She leaned over and picked up one, a bottle of sweet orange and jojoba oil. There was a stack of scented soaps, English Lavender, Gardenia Breeze, French Vanilla, and

Violette. Also on the shelf were French Vanilla and English Lavender bubble baths. In a glass-door cabinet that held towels and other linens, Rose saw silken body creams in Orange Crème and English Lavender, as well as body powder in French Vanilla. "That's a side business," said Alex.

"A side business? You make these?"

"No, you little imp. But the ingredients are grown on the ranch. My dad started the business years ago. A woman and her daughter created the products in a warehouse he provided. They no longer do it, but I'm in business with a new woman who does pretty much the same thing, but in a much more modern production plant. Her name is Camille Beckman. Maybe you've seen her products."

"Camille Beckman? Of course I know her products! They're elegant and only available in the finest stores." Rose leaned in to get a closer look at the bath soaps, wrapped in delicate paper and bearing the Camille Beckman trademark hand-tied silk rosebud. "That's you?"

"Well, no, it's her. I'm the silent business partner." Leading her out of the guest bedroom, he said, "And here's the main bedroom with the room-sized closet."

He opened the door and they stepped in. It was huge. It sat above the kitchen and dining area, so it was as big as those two spaces combined. There was a king-size bed, a dresser, and a wardrobe. A fireplace with a settee and two upholstered chairs were over near the glass double doors that led out to the deck. Rose looked at the wall adjacent to the bed and saw a set of about two dozen sketches, seemingly all of the same woman. As she stepped closer, she realized that many of them were rather lascivious. She looked at Alex quizzically.

"My girlfriend," he replied. When she frowned, he added, "It's a long story." He walked around to the far side of the bed. Between the bed and the wall with the sketches was the door leading to the closet. Alex stepped in first and turned on the light. "I don't really use this much. I hang some of my heavy stuff in here, like jackets and such, but other than that, it's pretty much empty." Rose couldn't believe what she was looking at. Two of the walls had poles on them for hanging clothes. One of these walls had two poles, one above the other. On the third wall was a long built-in dresser. On each side of the door were built in glass cabinets. In the center of the room was a huge island with a ceramic top and drawers underneath.

"This is incredible, Alex! I've never seen anything like it. Did you say it used to be a bedroom? Did your father do this for your mother?"

"For his first wife. But my mother got to enjoy it."

"One of these days you'll have to tell me about your father. He sounds interesting."

"I have some journals that will tell you everything you need to know about him. I learned things about him I never knew, until I read them."

"Sounds interesting."

"So, what do you think? Can the house be saved?"

"It's such a special house, Alex. We can restore it to its glory, with a modern touch!"

Chapter 7

March 1-8
Some 15,000 Latino high school students in Los Angeles walk out of classes to press their demand for a better education.

The day after Rose's arrival at the ranch, she and Alex drove into Riverside to browse the furniture stores. They had no firm idea of how they would redecorate the house, so they set out with open minds. Rose liked the idea of mid-century modern. Alex wasn't sure what that meant, but when she gave him a few examples he liked it.

By 1:00 they needed a break so they drove over to D'Elia's Grinders for lunch. While they ate, Rose suggested they pick up some copies of *Architectural Digest, Better Homes and Gardens*, and a variety of decorating magazines. She was beginning to formulate an idea in her mind of what the beautiful house could look like. They had agreed not to purchase furniture or anything else until they had drawn up the plans for the redecoration project. They agreed not to hire an interior decorator, but they probably would have to hire people to create cushions and drapes, and possibly people to design custom furniture.

Not only would they be redoing the downstairs, including the kitchen, they'd also be redoing Alex's bedroom. Rose loved the traditional furniture in there; maybe she could find a way to pull that into the lighter look of mid-century modern. She wasn't sure. She'd have to think about it.

After lunch they went on a magazine search, coming home with 14 magazines full of ideas. Rose spent the remainder of the afternoon looking through them, but she didn't even begin to make a dent in the pile. Before Heidi and Chloe left for the evening, she enlisted their input about what they thought the kitchen needed.

"New appliances!" said Chloe.

"A dishwasher!" intoned Heidi. "And new paint!" They were ecstatic that the kitchen would be updated, and even more thrilled that they were being consulted.

"New appliances, a dishwasher, and paint it will be," said Mac as he walked into the room. "But no macramé." They all laughed in agreement, although Rose added that she could make some nice plant hangers. "No," answered Alex. "No hippy kitchen." Rose gave him a playful punch in the arm.

Because they were both still full from lunch, Alex dismissed Heidi and Chloe, telling them they wouldn't need to make a dinner. But by 8:00 they were both getting hungry, so Alex reached into the freezer and pulled out two TV dinners. Each tray was divided into four sections. The largest section held slices of turkey and brown gravy; another section held mashed potatoes with butter; a third section was for green peas; and in the center of the tray was a small round depression that held sweet apples with sugar and cinnamon. While the TV dinners were in the oven, Alex asked Rose what she would like to drink. "Do you happen to have any Sangria?" she asked.

"As a matter of fact, I think I do," he answered as he reached into the back of the refrigerator. He poured her a glass of the fruity red wine, added ice and a slice of orange, and handed it to her. He poured himself a glass of Scotch and led her into the living room.

"I've been looking through some of the magazines we bought, but it's going to take me a long time to go through all of them. I'd like to take them home and really concentrate on what I'm seeing and hopefully begin to formulate a plan."

"I trust you, Rose. You're an artist."

"But not an interior decorator. But I will admit I have a lot of ideas about what we might do, and I'm excited about this project. What about the guest rooms? Will we include them in the makeover?"

"They haven't been touched in years. My parents didn't entertain much so they didn't get used. I think they still look exactly as they did when my dad was married to his first wife."

"You mentioned his ex-wife earlier. Did you ever meet her?"

"She wasn't his ex-wife. She died, and then he married my mother."

"Oh, I see. You didn't know about her until you read the journals?"

"I knew he had been married before. My mom talked about her a few times. I think my mom was jealous of her. Intimidated, anyway. I didn't think much about it until I became an adult and could empathize more with her. And then, when I read the journals, I actually felt a little sorry for my mom. Dede, that was her name, was an exceptional woman." He chuckled, "I even developed a crush on her myself."

"The pictures in your room. I noticed she was wearing old-fashion clothes and her hair was in that style women used to wear. Is that her?"

"Yes. My dad sketched her throughout their marriage. Again, I learned this from her journals."

"Would you consider letting me read them?"

"I'd love for you to read them! You'll get to know about my father, and maybe understand what makes me tick." They both chuckled. "You might also get a feel for the house. It's mentioned a lot in the journals."

"Can I take them home with me? I promise to return them."

"Well, there are boxfuls of them. Why don't you take a few at a time? I think you should start at the beginning. My dad even added a few entries of his own. And they're a great source of historical information from the turn of the century."

"I'd love to read them. I'll have my work cut out for me between the journals and the decorating magazines!"

He seated her at the large dining table and brought her a glass of white wine to replace the Sangria she had finished. He brought in the two TV dinners.

After dinner, they went upstairs. At the top of the stairs, Rose, feeling her Sangria and white wine, leaned in for a kiss. "Not tonight, honey," said Alex. He gave her a kiss on the forehead and opened the door to her room. "I'll see you in the morning."

Rose had an eddy of feelings whirling through her mine. *Not tonight? Not ever? How dare he humiliate me like that!* She felt foolish. Cheap. She had thrown herself at a man who rejected her. She crawled under the luxurious sheets and quilts and cried herself to sleep.

Alex was in a quandary. He wanted her so badly. Wanted to feel her, to taste her, to see her in a state of ecstasy. What was wrong with him? But he knew he had done the right thing. It was too early in their relationship, and she had had a glass of Sangria and two glasses of white wine. When he took her for the first time, he wanted it to be real, not an act emanating from too much wine. But oh, how he wanted her. He questioned himself until he fell asleep.

Chapter 8

March 6
Some 500 New York University students picket a university-sponsored recruiting event for the Dow Chemical Company, the principal manufacturer of napalm.

Rose had been poring through the magazines. She was getting a lot of ideas, although nothing had gelled yet. She was less interested in the decorating than she was in Dede's journals. In the last five days she had finished six of them and was nearing the end of the seventh. In between she looked at the magazines. And she thought about Alex.

The morning after he had left her in the hallway, humiliated, was awkward. He acted normal; she had a hard time breathing in front of him. She had packed up her belongings and was ready to go by 9:00.

"Wait a minute. Didn't you want to take some of the journals?"

"Yes. But I have to get going. I have to, uh, well, I have some things I need to do." He ran upstairs and came down with the first 10 journals. "I think you'll really like these." He carried them out to her car and put them in the trunk, which in a 911 Porsche was in the front, as the engine was in the back. She could hardly wait to get out of there and away from him. Had she been more mature, she would have talked to him about last night, about her feelings and his response; but she wasn't and so she didn't.

He called her just as she finished reading the fourth of Dede's journals. "That poor woman. Such horrible experiences she had when she was young."

"Yes," agreed Alex. "Keep reading." And so she had. In the journals, Dede had not yet met Mac, Alex's father. She was married to Cole and was living in Santa Monica. Cole seemed like a nice man. He was someone of importance in the railroad industry and was now (in the seventh journal) in Los Angeles heading up the Southern Pacific. He was a friend of the "Big Four," who Rose had read about in school. Leland Stanford, Collis Huntington, Mark Hopkins, and Charles Crocker had funded the building of the Central Pacific Railroad during the race to complete the transcontinental railroad back in the 1860s. It was rather exciting for Rose to be reading about someone to whom she had some ties, however tenuous they may be, to such an important event in history. She had never been much interested in history. She loved her art classes and her dance classes and the plays she had been in at school. She never thought much about history. But here, in these journals, were people who were living history. They were real people who had lived and made a difference. For the first time in her life, she was interested in history, in the people, both ordinary and extraordinary, who had shaped the country.

Four days went by and she hadn't heard from Alex again. She wondered what he was doing and why he hadn't called. She wished it wasn't so improper for a woman to call a man, otherwise she would have called him. But her mother would have died! Two more days went by and still no word from him. She finished the 10 journals she had brought home with her and had leafed through more design magazines. She was depressed. She went into the kitchen and took down the cookie tin from the top shelf of the cupboard. Opening it, she smelled the sweet aroma of the dried weed. She took out a small square of paper to roll it in, pinched both ends, and went out to her backyard deck. She had become pretty proficient over the past year in rolling her own weed and was proud of how well it had turned out. It was slender and straight, not bulky and bumpy as other peoples' often were. She lit it and inhaled deeply. She sat there, smoking and thinking about Alex. By the time she had finished the joint, she no longer cared much about him. She went indoors, grabbed a bag of potato chips, and sat down to watch television.

The phone rang. "Hello?"

"Miss Lefebre. What have you been up to?" She could not believe that he was acting like everything was so normal.

"Reading."

"Oh yeah? The journals?"

"Uh-ha. And magazines."

"Getting any good ideas?"

"How dare you disappear for a week and then call up and act like nothing's wrong!"

Alex was surprised by this sudden outburst of anger. He was unsure how to move forward. "I was up in Wyoming. Why are you so upset?"

"You should have told me you were going away! I've been sitting here day after day wondering where you were!"

"Why did I need to tell you? For your approval? Honey, I haven't been accountable to anyone since I left the Marine Corp, and I'm not about to start getting your permission for things I need to do."

She hung up on him. How dare he speak to her like that! He called her honey. So condescending. It would be nice to have a man call her honey as an endearment, but that's not what this had been. It was demeaning. The phone rang again.

"Look," he continued. "I'm a little out of practice here. I've lived on my own my whole life. I'm tripping over my own feet, my tongue, and anything else a lout can trip over. I'm sorry. I should have been more thoughtful."

"Yes, you should have been."

"You sound a little drowsy. Did I catch you sleeping?"

"No," she answered as she sat up straighter.

"Oh, well, I was wondering if you'd like to get together. I have a contractor coming by to talk about wiring, plumbing, centralized heating and air, and other infrastructure updates. I'm interested in your ideas about the house. Think you could come up here again?"

"I guess. When would you like me to come?"

"Anytime. Now? Tomorrow? As soon as you can."

"Tomorrow. I'll see you then. Bye." She replaced the receiver into the phone cradle.

Alex knew he was in trouble. It honestly had never crossed his mind to tell her he was leaving for a week. He had been busy making plans with the hands, getting the four horse trailers hitched to the trucks, and taking care of everything else he needed to do to get ready for the horse roundup. He would have to make it up to her. He wondered why she sounded so bad and hoped she wasn't getting sick.

It was 4:00 when she pulled up in front of the sprawling house and Alex came out of the front door. "Hi, beautiful. I hope you didn't hit much traffic." She looked gorgeous, wearing tight black pants that flared wide at the bottom and a frilly silk blouse. Her hair was in a long ponytail hanging down her back, juxtaposing a look of innocence with that of a sexy allure. He wondered if she had any idea how attractive she was.

"It was fine. Can you help me with some of these books?" She opened the bonnet and Alex scooped up the 10 journals and all the magazines. He took them into the living room and set them on the large coffee table in front of the fireplace.

"What can I get you to drink? I know after a drive like that you need to relax. Anyway, I always do."

"A glass of that white wine would be nice."

"You got it." He went into the kitchen and poured a glass of chilled wine, then sat next to her on the sofa. "So, any ideas?"

"Yes, actually. I've put together this concept board for you, to see how you like the colors so far. He noticed she was carrying a large sheet of poster board when she walked in but had no idea what it was. On it, she had glued pictures of furniture she had cut out of some of the magazines. She had also made swirls of complementing and contrasting colors, presumably from her own oil paints: shades of greens and blues, turquoise, orange, yellow, gold, and various pinks. The board held swatches of cottons, silks, and damasks, all in a variety of colors, lengths, solids, and prints. She walked over and stood it up on the mantle above the fireplace so they could both get a good look at it. They both stood up, next to each other behind the sofa.

"What is it? Are these the things we're going to use to redecorate the house?"

Rose laughed. "No, silly!" It's a collage of ideas. I love the idea of doing it up in mid-century modern. And of course the trending colors these days are turquoise with complementary blues and greens, and contrasting oranges and golds. I just want you to take a look at it and tell me if the board pleases you or offends you."

Alex wasn't looking at the board. He was looking at her. "I'm in awe, Rose. I love how your mind works. I love your artistic vision. I had no idea you would put together something like this."

"But do you like it, or would you rather I go back to the drawing board?"

"I really like it. And I like some of the furniture you've chosen from the magazines." Pointing to a round, turquoise sofa, he asked, "What do you call these things again?"

"Sectionals. They're all the rage now, especially in mid-century modern."

He was just about ready to take her in his arms and kiss her, when Chloe walked in and noticed the concept board. "Is that it? Is that what this place is going to look like? I love it! Heids, come in here and see this!" Heidi came in and walked up to the poster. "Wow," she exclaimed, "this is bitchin'! Oh, sorry, Mr. MacKenzie. When do we get started?"

"There are a lot of decisions to be made first. Like colors, fabrics, furniture, and more basically, which room should we begin in?" Rose was becoming more and more anxious as she thought about it. It was going to be a monumental job.

"The kitchen!" chimed in both Heidi and Chloe.

"We could," said Rose, looking to Alex as though asking his approval. "There are probably fewer decisions to be made in there, so it might be a good place for us to start."

Heidi and Chloe giggled with excitement. Then Heidi said, "Dinner will be ready in about a half hour. Good for you?"

"Good for us," Rose and Alex answered in unison.

Rose walked over to the fireplace to remove the board. "No, leave it there," said Alex.

"But it's covering up this nice impressionist-style painting." As she took a closer look she said, "Who painted it?"

"Monet."

"No! I've never seen it in any catalogues. Is it a reproduction? Where did you get it?"

"He was a friend of my father. He painted it for him as a gift. If you look out this window toward the southeast, you'll get a view of the landscape in the painting."

Rose hadn't heard anything beyond the fact that his father had been a friend of Monet. "Are you kidding me?"

"No, come over here to the window and you'll see it. It looks just like the painting."

"Yes, but I mean, your father knew Monet? How did that happen?"

"My dad went to medical school in Paris. He actually knew many of the Impressionists. Keep reading the journals. You'll see." Rose realized her mouth was hanging open and quickly closed it. She took the poster down so she could get a better look at this original Monet which had been painted for Mac MacKenzie.

They moved to the dining room table and sat down for dinner, Alex at the head of the table and Rose in the first seat on his left. Heidi and Chloe had made a fabulous meal of chicken in gravy, biscuits, green beans, and mashed potatoes. "This chicken is delicious, but it tastes different than the chicken my mom makes," said Rose.

"That's because it's natural. We raise our own chickens, just like we raise our own cattle and hogs and vegetables. Chicken you buy in the store has been shot up with steroids and antibiotics to make them grow fat quickly. Our chickens live a happy life and get fat naturally, roaming free all around the barnyard. You'll get used to it."

"I like it already. And I really like the fact that it's natural."

After dinner they went upstairs, Alex carrying Rose's suitcase and an armload of the journals. He opened the door to her room, which once again had vases of freshly cut flowers on the dresser and on the table by the window. Alex set the suitcase on the rack made for the purpose and set the journals on the dresser.

Rose was at the window looking out at the courtyard and swimming pool. He walked over to her, turned her toward him, and gave her a kiss. It wasn't merely a kiss as a greeting; it was a long, sensuous, possessive kiss. When he pulled away from her, he looked into her eyes and said, "I've been wanting to do that since the first night I met you."

Her breathing had quickened. She looked into his eyes and leaned in for another kiss, which he generously bestowed. "I had no idea," she stammered. "You gave me no hints. But I've wanted it too, that is, when I'm not infuriated at you." He smiled at her. "I won't infuriate you tonight. Far from it," and he kissed her again.

"My goodness," she moaned, "but you sure know how to kiss a girl."

"Let me show you what else I know how to do." He picked her up and carried her to the side of the bed, where he set her down on her two feet. He began to rub her back and her arms. "Do you have any idea how sexy this blouse is? I've been wanting to touch it since you stepped out of the car. I want to feel you through it, and I want to take it off of you and see your beautiful body." He began to unbutton the blouse.

Rose was finding it hard to breathe. She had never experienced this kind of lovemaking. She had been with a number of men; after all, she was 32 years old. But she had never experienced this. If she had been able to think, which she couldn't at the time, she would have realized that having sex is very different than making love. Alex was making love to her.

When he was finished unbuttoning the blouse, he slid it off her arms and let it drop to the floor. He unhooked her bra, gently slid it off and let it drop to the floor also. He stood back and looked at her. He let out a slow whistle. "Miss Rose Lefebre, you are one beautiful woman." He stepped forward and gave her another long, sensuous kiss, this time lightly touching her nipples as he did so. When the kiss was over, Rose began to unbutton his shirt and untuck it from his Levi's. She spread open the sides of the shirt and looked at his chest. She placed her hands on it and felt the hair, course and somewhat curly. She stepped closer, wrapping her arms around his warm body and placing her head on his chest. She could feel his heart beat slow and steady, and she felt his strength.

After a few minutes, he tilted her head up for another kiss. "What do you say we each lose our pants and crawl into that bed?" She laughed, a quietly muffled chuckle. Right in the middle of lovemaking he has to say something funny. She had never known anyone like Alex.

She crawled in between the sheets, which smelled clean and fresh, like they'd been dried on a clothesline outdoors. Before he took his pants off, he asked, "Protection?"

"Protection? Oh, uh, no. I usually leave that up to the man."

"You're not on the pill?"

"Well, you know, being Catholic and all."

"You little hypocrite. I'll be right back." Alex went to his bedroom and was back within a minute. He took off his pants, slid in beside her and immediately began to kiss her. He kissed her face, her eyelids, her cheeks, her neck, all the while his hands feeling her breasts. Her nipples were hard, and he gently squeezed them before exploring them with his tongue. She arched her back and moaned. "Oh yes, Rose, enjoy every minute of it," he answered.

"Alex, I don't think I can wait any longer."

"Oh yes you can, darling. Yes you can." He moved his hand down her body, stopping to knead her hip. She moaned. He slid his hand from her hip to the inside of her thigh. She moaned again and took in a deep breath. His fingers explored her most sensitive parts and she cried out, "I can't wait anymore!" He positioned himself on top of her and entered her. Their bodies moved together in an orchestrated rhythm, but only for a few minutes before they both experienced the climax. He laid on top of her propped on his elbows and continued to kiss her passionately. When they were both utterly satisfied, he looked her in the eyes and smiled, then rolled off of her.

Rose rolled on to her side and rested her head against his chest. "What did you do to me, Alex?"

"Not nearly as much as I'd have liked to, Rose." He kissed the top of her head. "I think we're going to have to work up a little more stamina."

She laughed. "I am, that's for sure. I don't know about you." Alex gently rubbed her back and she soon fell asleep.

At about midnight Rose woke up. She rubbed her hand on his chest, her fingers playing with the coarse hair. Alex woke up and they played the game all over again, with the same results. They fell back asleep and slept until the morning light woke them up.

Alex got out of bed, encouraging Rose to stay under the warm blankets. He came back with a tray on which there were a carafe of coffee, two mugs, toast, jam, and slices of apple. There was also a vase with a rose bud in it. "Chloe helped me," he explained. He got back into bed, both of them sitting up, with the tray on his lap.

"I know I'm a hypocrite. But a girl has to draw the line somewhere."

"You don't need to explain. These are confusing times, Rose. Everyone is still deciding which rules to keep, which to bend, and which to break. I was teasing you."

"Teasing, yes, but you were right."

Alex leaned over and kissed her cheek. "I'm going to take a quick shower and go out to the corral. I want to check on my new horses. Would you like to come with me?"

"No. I think I'll take a luxurious bath and then read the next journal, if you're ok with that."

"Sure. I'll get out a few more for you before I leave." With that, he kissed her a quick kiss on her toast-and-jam mouth and left.

Chapter 9

March 13
*Atlantic Richfield and Humble Oil (now Exxon Mobil)
announce the discovery of an oil field beneath Prudhoe
Bay Alaska, the largest oil and natural-gas discovery in
North American History.*

Rose stayed at Alex's house for several days, reading, designing, making love, laughing, talking, getting to know him, and falling in love. On the way back to Laguna Beach, she stopped in Placentia to visit her mother and father. Her mother was in the kitchen and her father was in his office. "Well, you look like a happy woman," exclained her mother.

"Mom, I think I'm in love," answered Rose, seriously.

Her mom wiped her hands on a dish towel and came over to give her a sincere hug. "I can tell. You're radiant! Let me pour some coffee and we'll go into the living room and you can tell me all about the man you're in love with." Rose moved into the living room and her mother, Edna Ryan Lefebre, followed with two cups of hot coffee, black, the way they both liked them. "So let me hear all about it," she said again.

"Well, I've actually known him for a couple of months now, but I haven't mentioned him because, well, quite frankly, he infuriated me. And he's nothing like anyone else I've ever known."

"What? Not like Jimmy Dinsmore?" At this they both laughed. Rose had a crush on Jimmy Dinsmore in the 8th grade. She was attracted to him because he smoked and got in fights. She thought he was a misunderstood bad boy. She went to the 8th grade graduation dance with him, but her father had to pick her up early because Jimmy got in a fight and was kicked out of the dance. After her first day of high school, Rose realized there were a lot better fish in the sea and quickly forgot about Jimmy Dinsmore, who for some reason never started high school, at least not her high school.

Still laughing, Rose said, "No, Mom, not at all like Jimmy Dinsmore. I met him at the opening of that local history museum I was working on. His name is Alex MacKenzie, and he's the most amazing man I've ever known!"

"Alex MacKenzie. Out near Riverside? Is he related to the MacKenzies of the MacKenzie Ranch?"

"He IS the MacKenzie Ranch, Mom. There's only been two of them, his father who started it, and now him."

"So he's what I would call famous. Everyone in Southern California knows about the MacKenzie Ranch."

"I met him that night, and we went out to dinner. I thought we were going to go somewhere fancy but he took me to a sandwich place." Rose continued to tell her mother about the embarrassing mistake she had made upon meeting the man who had funded the museum, how he had treated her like a spoiled child, and how, ultimately, she had fallen in love with him. She told her about her painting that he had bought, and about the big decorating job ahead. She told her about the huge house, about Heidi and Chloe, and about spending the past several days there. Her mother, who was a devout Catholic, as was her Peruvian grandmother who had raised her, would not have approved of anyone else spending the night with a man. But she knew her daughter was a free spirit, and Edna hoped that at 32 Rose would find someone and settle down. If it took staying in a man's house without being married to him to yield that result, she was willing to overlook it.

"How old is he, honey? His father started that ranch back in the 1800s."

"He's 48. I know, a lot older than me. He was even in the war, Mom. I'm talking about World War II!"

"Well, let's see. You're 32, so he's 16 years older than you. That's not really so bad. How old was his father when he was born, for heaven's sake?"

Rose laughed. "He was pretty old. I think he said 70, or close to it."

"You know, honey, I think my grandmother knew him. His name is mentioned a couple of times in her memoir. He and Alex's mother." Edna went upstairs and came down with the memoir. "Here, why don't you take this. You need to read it anyway. You need to know your own ancestry."

Rose took the book and gently laid it on her lap. It had aged over the years and she didn't want it to fall apart. Rose told her mother about Dede's journals. By now she had read 17 of them. Dede and Cole had been to Mac's grand opening of his own railway, Cole had been a disappointment as a husband and had badly mistreated her, and she was now teaching at the University of Southern California. Rose was eager to read the next 10 journals, which she had brought home with her. She wanted to get to the part where Dede and Mac fell in love.

Edna stood to get more coffee, but Rose said she wanted to get home. "Rose, darling, I'm so happy for you. He does sound like a wonderful man, and I'm looking forward to meeting him."

"I can't wait for you to meet him, Mom. You're going to love him!"

"If you do, I will." She gave her a long parting hug.

For the first few days she was home, she couldn't pull herself away from the journals. But today she knew she had to do something more productive. She drove down the hill to her studio. She rented a space in the southwest corner of a second-floor loft, where she had good light for most of the day. She busied herself stapling canvas to various sized frames, although she didn't really have any inspiring thoughts about what to put on those canvasses. Her painting was like that. Inspiration came in spurts. Sometimes she couldn't get her ideas onto the canvas fast enough; other times, like now, her ideas were dormant. She also loved to work with clay. She had made many bowls, vases, dishes, and mugs for herself and for her family and friends. Maybe she was more in the mood to do that.

She decided she would make Alex a plate with curved edges, not quite a bowl and not quite just a plate. The pottery room, which was available on a first come first served basis, was not in use this afternoon, so she set to work setting out her supplies. While she was doing this, Kyle stepped in. "I thought I saw your car out there," he said. Kyle was her friend who rented the house where she had taken Alex. She hadn't seen him since that night.

"Oh, hi Kyle. What's going on?"

"Been working. Not all of us are so privileged to indulge our artistic whims whenever we want to. Some of us have to work." It always irked Rose when her friends said things like this, which was often. She knew she was privileged and she didn't think it was her fault they weren't. Kyle had completed two years of college but had dropped out in his third year, telling people that he didn't need a piece of paper to prove he was intelligent. Rose acknowledged that he was intelligent. He read Bertrand Russell, George Orwell, Maxim Gorky, and Karl Marx. He was constantly quoting Nietzsche. One of his favorites was, "There are no facts, only interpretations." Rose had contemplated this quote often, never sure she agreed with it. She was quite certain Alex wouldn't agree with it.

"We have art in order not to die of the truth," said Kyle now, once again quoting Nietzche. "What are you making now, my Porsche-driving friend, in order not to die?"

He was getting on her nerves. "I'm not sure. Maybe a plate. I'm not inspired to paint right now, but I am inspired to create. I thought some time down here might be a good way to release some creativity."

"Oh. I just came to pick up some supplies. Hey, I'm having some friends in tonight. You oughta join us."

"Maybe. I'll see how I do here, then I might come over for awhile."

"Suit yourself. You know where I live. BYOB." With that back-handed invitation, he left. Rose felt like she was moving between two worlds. Her friends, like Kyle, no longer held the pull on her like they used to. She preferred to live in Alex's world, which quite honestly was similar to the one in which she had grown up. Her brothers had been in the war, went to college, and held very traditional beliefs. But she had been attracted to artists, the free thinkers, the risk takers. A brief thought occurred to her: what risk were these people taking? Hadn't it been people like her brothers and Alex who had taken the greatest risk? She pushed these thoughts out of her mind and got to work on the plate.

Three hours later, the workspace was cleaner than she had found it and the plate was drying. She'd put it in the kiln in a couple of days. She drove home and got ready to go over to Kyle's.

As she walked in the door, she found the setting as she usually found it. About seven or eight friends sitting on his floor in a circle. The music was loud. Tonight it was the Doors, and right now it was the long riff of *Light My Fire*. The drinks had been set up in the kitchen. She stepped in to set her own bottle of wine on the counter. All of a sudden, she had a sickening feeling of betrayal, that she was betraying Alex by bringing white wine to this get-together. White wine was what she drank when she was with him, not when she was with these people. She usually drank a beer or a wine cooler when she was here. Nevertheless, she poured some wine into a plastic cup and joined the circle. There was a plastic cup on the table in front of her that held cash. She put in $2.00. Two joints were moving around the circle. The air was redolent with the sweet aroma of marijuana. The joint was passed to her and she took a toke from it, not nearly as long a toke as she usually took. She inhaled deeply and passed the joint to the next person. Slowly, she exhaled.

About five minutes later, the second joint was passed to her, and she repeated her action. She had shared the weed about four times when the door was kicked open. Five policemen rushed in, two with their guns drawn. "Nobody move!" one of them shouted. One of the policemen took pictures, while two held their guns on the group, and the other two circled behind the group, handcuffing each person in turn. "You're under arrest for the possession and sale of marijuana, a felony." Following the Supreme Court ruling of 1966, one of the policeman read from a card, "You have the right to remain silent. Anything you say can and will be used against you in a court of law. You have the right to an attorney. If you cannot afford one, one will be appointed to you."

Rose was petrified. She realized she was going to jail. As they were roughly escorted out of the house, Rose heard Joaquim, one of her friends, mumble, "Bummer." The men were put in the back of a panel wagon; Rose and the other two women were put in the back of a squad car. She knew one of the women, Vicki, but did not know the other one. She wanted to cry, but noticed the other women seemed to be taking it in stride, so she tried to hold her tears back.

When they arrived at the police station, the men were taken to a cell. Rose and the other women were escorted down a long hallway and put in a cell together on the opposite side of the building from the men's cell. At least her handcuffs were taken off. She was shaking. She had to go to the bathroom. The cell had a stainless steal toilet and a matching basin, but it was dirty. Not only that, but it was not shielded from view. She couldn't bring herself to use it.

Rose knew enough to understand that a felony was serious. Possession drew a sentence of two to ten years in prison. Sale was punishable by five to ten years to life. But she hadn't sold it. *Oh, wait*, she thought. *I put $2.00 in the cup. I bought it. Is that the same?* She sat on the bench and let the tears flow.

She woke up at 1:30 A.M. because she had to urinate so badly. She took a look at the urinal and couldn't believe that she had to use it. When she was done, she sat back down on the bench. The other two girls were asleep on the other bench. *What about bail?* She wondered. *Shouldn't I get to put up some kind of bail and get out of here?* 2:00. 3:00. She was awakened at half past 7:00 by a policewoman who had come to get them for arraignment.

"Officer, how long will I have to stay? Can't I pay bail or something and leave?"

"That's up to the arraignment judge, Ma'am. That's where we're going now."

"But how long will that take?"

"I don't know. I don't know where your case is on the docket."

"Do I get an attorney?"

"Do you want one?"

"I don't know. I've never been arrested. What happens? Am I going to be sentenced now?

"Look, the judge will take a look at your case, at your past record, at your work history, etc. He'll decide if bail will be set and if so, how much it'll be." Rose didn't have a past record, but neither did she have much of a work resume. She picked up work in the art world as it interested her, never anything steady. Would that count against her?

They were led into a court room and seated in a holding area behind a thick plexiglass screen. Besides her and her friends, there were about 20 other people in there, some of them dressed in orange jumpsuits. Her eyes darted from side to side, to the judge, to some men who appeared to be attorneys, to the bailiff, and back to the people in the holding cell with her. She had never been so frightened in her life. Sixteen people were called before she was. Some of them had attorneys and some of them didn't. She had stopped listening to the proceedings after the first few people. It was monotonous and she wasn't sure if they were in there for arraignment or sentencing. Rose's brother was an attorney. She should have called him. Oh no, she couldn't have done that. *He mustn't ever know about this. Nobody can ever know about this!*

When her name was called she was led up to an area where she faced the judge. He read the charges against her. "Do you understand the charges, Miss Lefebre?"

"Yes, your honor."

$2000 bail. Next?"

She was led out of the courtroom and back to her cell. *$2000? Did I hear that right? How am I going to get my hands on $2000?* The policewoman told her that soon she would be able to make a phone call to arrange for bail and have someone come and get her. She knew she couldn't call her family's attorney who oversaw her trust fund. Any time she needed to access the fund, she'd made an appointment with him and had to justify the expense. No, she couldn't call him. Rose spent the next hour agonizing over who she would call. In the end, there was only one person she could call.

"Alex?" As soon as she heard his voice she burst into tears.

"Rose, are you alright? Rose, honey, try to stop crying and tell me what's wrong. Are you ok? Is it your parents?"

She took several deep breaths and tried to calm down enough to tell him where she was. She told him. It all came out in one long sentence. "And I don't know how to get my money to pay for bail. I don't want anyone in my family to know what's happened." She was crying again. He asked how much she needed, where specifically she was, and told her to sit tight, that he'd be there as soon as possible.

Alex had been arrested once. It was the year he was discharged from the Marine Corp. He had gotten into a fight in a bar and had broken a bottle over some sailor's head. Alex was arrested on several charges and had to spend three nights in a jail cell. It had been a Friday night and the courts didn't open again until Monday. He knew how bad jail cells were. It broke his heart to think of Rose being anywhere near one. He also knew the process. So he went to the bank, got a cashier's check, and drove to Laguna Beach. He was so disappointed in Rose.

Rose came from the back of the building to meet him in the lobby of the police station. She took one look at Alex and saw the disappointment in his eyes. He put his arm around her and led her out to his truck. Opening the door for her, he asked, "I suppose you want to go straight home?"

"Yes."

"Have you eaten?"

"They brought in a tray but I couldn't eat it."

"Do you want to stop and get something?"

"No. I just want to go home."

When they got to her house, she started to get out of the truck. "No, wait," he said, "I'll help you out."

"No, it's ok. You can leave."

"I'm not leaving. We're going to talk." He got out, walked around to her side, and helped her out of the truck.

While she took a shower, he fixed something to eat. He found a pound of ground beef that looked fairly fresh. He also found a can of beans, an onion, and some cheese. He made burritos, which were fairly easy to assemble. As he was finishing the assembly, Rose appeared in fresh clothing and wet hair. She looked stunning. She was wearing tight Levi's and a white gauze blouse. Two draw strings could have been tied at the neck, but she had left them hanging. She looked innocent.

Alex put the plates on the kitchen dinette table and held a chair out for her, then he sat down. "Thank you for doing this, Alex."

"What? The food?"

"Yes, and for everything. I know I ruined everything between us."

"I thought I wanted to spend the rest of my life with you, Rose. But this isn't the kind of girl I want. Not someone who smokes dope and ends up with a felony on her record."

"I know. I just said I know I've ruined everything. Please leave now, Alex."

"What were you thinking?"

She hung her head. She had taken a bite of the burrito but now found she could neither chew nor swallow it. She gagged, got up, and spit it out in the sink. "I guess I wasn't thinking. I hadn't seen these people in some time, not since you and I were there, and I felt bad that I had been ignoring them. I didn't know the police were going to kick in the door!"

"I see. So you thought it was ok to go over there and smoke dope, as long as the police left you alone?"

"Yes. No. I don't know. I didn't really think about it."

"Rose, you're not a reckless teenager. You're a 32-year-old woman. You knew what you were doing and you knew the consequences of getting caught. Now you've been caught. What are you going to do?"

"I don't know." She started to cry again.

Alex told her about his own experience getting arrested years ago. "But the charges were all misdemeanors. I paid a fine and that was the end of it. Possession and sale of marijuana are felonies, Rose. You may have to go to prison." She started to cry harder. He led her to the living room sofa and held her while she lay on his lap and cried. The tears flowed freely. He petted her head and back all the while.

When she was all cried out, he stood up. "I need to finish eating. I wish you would eat something. You're skinny as a rail and you need some nourishment in you. You've been through a lot." He brought their plates into the living room. He finished his burrito, made another, and finished that. She took two tiny bites of hers and pushed it aside.

It was getting dark. Alex went out and locked his truck. Rose thought he was leaving and was surprised when he came back inside. "I'm going to stay here with you tonight. I don't want you to be alone." Just then the telephone rang. She looked at him as for permission to answer it. When she got no response either way, she answered it.

It was Vicki. "Could you believe those pigs!" Alex could hear her voice coming through the receiver. "How dare they come into a private home and arrest us! They had no right to do that! And sale? Nobody was selling anything! Kyle's gonna fight it. We're all going to fight it!"

"Vicki, I don't want to talk about it. Not right now anyway. I'm hanging up now." She hung up the phone.

"They did have a right, you know," said Alex.

"Can we not talk about it anymore tonight?"

"Fair enough. You've got to be exhausted."

"I'll get you some blankets."

"Blankets? Where am I sleeping?"

"I thought you'd want to sleep out here."

"No, I'm sleeping with you." They went into the bedroom. Rose disappeared into the bathroom and changed into a nightgown. Alex stripped down to his boxer shorts and crawled into bed. The waterbed would take some getting used to. When Rose joined him, he held her in his arms, her head resting on his chest, and they both fell asleep.

In the morning he took her back to Kyle's place to retrieve her car. She had put on the same clothes she was wearing after her shower yesterday. Once again, he marveled to himself about how she could look innocent and sexy at the same time. When they got back to her house, he said, "Pack some things enough for a couple of weeks."

"What? Alex, I'm not the girl you want. You said so yourself."

"I'm not giving up on you yet, Rose. But I think I'm going to have to keep you close so I can keep an eye on you. Pack up."

Rose set out food and water for CaliCat and asked her neighbor to check on her and water the plants every few days. She didn't know how long she'd be gone.

As they were pulling out of her driveway, Rose remembered the plate she had left drying in the studio. It still needed to go into the kiln. She asked Alex if they could stop by so she could get it before anyone ruined it. Before pottery went into the kiln, it was extremely fragile. When they got there, he went in with her. He had never been in an art studio. The smells and the clutter were offensive to his sense of order, but he stayed close to Rose while she got the plate and took it upstairs to her space. He was glad to see that her space was tidy and organized. "What do you do with it now?" he asked.

"It needs to go in the kiln."

"How long will that take?"

"Not long, but it will have to bake for a day. I can't do it right now. I'll just leave it here until I get back."

"Why don't you bring it with you? You can finish it at my house."

"I can't do that. I need a kiln."

"We'll buy one."

Rose laughed. "No, silly. You have to have a special place to put it. You can't just bring it into the house and set it up."

"I have a good place for it. Bring your plate and whatever else you need."

Rose was somewhat stunned. "Well, what color would you like it to be? I'm making it for you, you know."

He was touched and had an overwhelming desire to kiss her. He took her in his arms and gave her a warm, heartfelt, and sensuous kiss. "I don't know what I'm going to do with you, you Rose. You choose the color, and let's get on the road."

Chapter 10

March 16
New York Senator Robert F. Kennedy enters the race for the Democratic presidential nomination, saying McCarthy's showing in New Hampshire "has proven how deep are the present divisions within our party and country." It "is now unmistakably clear that we can change these disastrous, divisive policies only by changing the men who make them."

They had been back at the ranch for several days. Rose knew of an art supply store near Riverside where they could order a kiln, so they had stopped in there on their way back from Laguna Beach. Alex had told the salesman they would need it to be delivered and installed. It was going to be delivered today.

There were two guest houses on the ranch. Heidi and Chloe shared one; the other one had been vacant for years. Alex told Rose she could have it and use it as an art studio whenever she was at the ranch. He called in a few of the hands to clean it out and give it a new coat of paint. Rose said it was perfect, except it was too bad that big tree prevented more light from getting in. The tree was removed. They had been back to the art supply store for canvases, oils, brushes, easels, turpentine, pottery supplies, and anything else she would need to work in a fully-stocked studio.

She glazed the plate/bowl with yellow and white colors, swirling them in circles around the center of the plate and out to the edges. As soon as the kiln was delivered, she set the plate in it, added the firing cones, and left it to bake. Alex came in and found her gleefully in her element. He had brought her a large vase of tree branches overburdened with orange blossoms and set it on the round table in the main room. "Alex, they're beautiful! And they smell wonderful! I'm going to make some containers and put hanging plants in them. I'll make the hangers too," she excitedly told him.

"That's fine. Just keep them in here. I don't want any of that hippy stuff in the house."

"It's not hippy, Alex. It's artistic."

"Whatever. Here, sit down and let's talk." They had been to a furniture store and purchased a loveseat off the showroom floor. It was upholstered in large pink, red, and orange flowers. It was colorful, overstuffed, and very comfortable. It fit into the studio environment perfectly. "We need to talk about the future."

"OK," she replied. "If you're going to dump me as your girlfriend, can I still have access to my studio?"

"I'm not going to dump you, Rose. In 48 years, you're the only woman I think I've really loved. The only one I can't get out of my mind."

"You love me, Alex?" she asked, and tears filled her eyes.

"Yes, honey, I love you. I want the two of us to grow old together."

"Don't you mean 'older'?"

They both chuckled. "OK, older." Then he got serious. "You're going to have to give up that life. There's no place for that in my life."

"Alex, I've been doing a lot of thinking. I don't want that kind of life anymore. Those people aren't true friends. They say insulting things to me because I live off a trust fund. I've never said anything offensive to them, but they think nothing of offending me."

"Not only are they not your friends, honey, they're socialists, commies for damn sake! I saw Kyle's books when I was there. A bunch of left-wing propaganda. You don't want that kind of life. Your parents raised you to be better than that."

Rose lowered her eyes and said quietly, "I know."

"But I do think you need to start thinking about something and someone beside yourself. You and I are privileged, Rose, but that doesn't mean we can turn our backs on those less fortunate. Do you know what I mean?"

"Yes. What do you want me to do?"

"It's not what I want. You're going to have to find your own way to give back to a society that has allowed your family to be successful. Yes, I know it's the American way, and I know your parents and grandparents worked hard for what they got. But let's face it, you didn't, and it's time you started doing something to help others."

"You think I'm self-centered, don't you?"

"Yes, I do. Give it some thought. Find something you can do to help someone else." They sat there in silence for a while. Then Alex continued, "And we have to take care of this other business. You need an attorney. Why don't you call your brother?"

"No! No one in my family can know about this!"

"Would you like me to call my attorney and see what he recommends?"

She looked up at him, "Yes, please." Then she added, "Alex, I'm going to be a better person. My parents and brothers are wonderful people, but they spoiled me rotten. Nothing was ever expected of me, and I never pushed myself to do or be anything other than what I wanted. But you'll see. I want to be better, more giving, more mature, for you."

"Do you love me, Rose?"

"With all my heart." He pulled her close to him and they sat like that for some time. Finally, he told her he had to go out to the groves and check on a few things. They stood up, he gave her a warm hug and kissed her on the forehead, then left. Oddly, she felt better. One would think she'd take offense to being scolded about her selfishness, but she actually felt good. She felt as though she had direction now, a path to the future, and that future would have a purpose. Moreover, Alex would be in her life.

Chapter 11

March 19
Hundreds of students take over the administration building at Howard University in Washington, D.C., seeking a greater voice in student discipline and the curriculum.

Heidi and Chloe were preparing dinner and Alex was in his office. Rose entered carrying a nicely wrapped present. "What do you have there?" inquired Alex.

"A gift for the man in my life," she answered as she handed it to him.

"Let's go sit in the living room where I can unwrap it." They sat side by side on the settee. He unwrapped it, suspecting he knew what it was, but he didn't know what the finished product would look like. He was surprised when he took it out of the box, not realizing she had painted it in yellow. It had swirls of yellow and white going around and around from the center outward. "It's beautiful, Rose. Full of sunshine, just like you." He leaned over and gave her a quick kiss. "But it's too nice to actually use. What will we do with it?"

"Use it, silly. I made it for you to use. You can put anything in it. Nuts, candy, dried flowers. Or you can put water in it and float some flowers in it. Orange blossoms, maybe. Or Heidi could load it up with mashed potatoes!"

"Well, I'll have to think about that. Really, Rose, your talent is amazing. Thank you."

"Thank you, Alex. For everything you've given me. Especially another chance."

"I did that because I don't want to lose you."

Heidi interrupted them. "Dinner is ready. If you'd like me to keep it warm awhile longer, I can."

"No, no, we're ready. Aren't we Rose?"

Dinner was a ham and cheese and sliced potato casserole. It had some kind of a secret ingredient, maybe marjoram with mustard, that gave it a scrumptious aroma. Asparagus spears were on a platter. There was also a lovely green salad with homemade Green Goddess dressing, tossed with basil and thyme. The girls had made two loaves of homemade bread. "I'm starving!" proclaimed Rose. Alex looked at Heidi and Chloe and the three of them broke out in laughter.

Later, Alex explained to Rose that he always encouraged the girls to make enough to take home dinner for themselves. They were young but had worked for him for three years. He hired Heidi first, and after a couple of months she approached him to ask if perhaps he might approve of a second housekeeper, as the house was large (even with all the guest rooms closed up) and there was laundry, cooking, and even vegetable gardening to keep up with. Once he approved the second housekeeper, she jumped right in with the request to hire her friend, Chloe. He had been skeptical at first, not knowing how two friends would work out. He predicted that they would spend most of their time talking instead of working. But he had been surprised at their work ethic. Before them, he had used a number of maid services. They showed up once a week, always a different crew, and because he never really got to know any of them, he didn't trust any of them. He had been cooking dinners for himself, mostly frozen TV dinners. He was extremely happy with Heidi and Chloe. He wondered to himself if they were more than friends. Neither one of them seemed to have a boyfriend. But it didn't matter to him either way. They were good workers, great cooks, and trustworthy.

Chapter 12

April 3
Some 1000 men return their draft cards to government offices all over the country.

"It's OK, CaliCat. Mama has you now." Cali was on her lap as she drove her Porsche, following Alex back to the ranch. She had the radio tuned to KRLA, listening to Stevie Wonder's *I Was Made to Love Her.* They had gone back to Rose's house, where she packed up a few more items of clothing, including a suit she could wear to meet with the attorney tomorrow. Before she had left several weeks ago, she had made arrangements for her neighbor to water the plants once a week and to set food out for CaliCat every few days. CaliCat could come in and out of the cat door which had been installed in the door leading out to the backyard. She found plenty to eat out there, but Rose had asked her neighbor to make sure she had a supply of dry food and water available for Cali. But now, she wanted CaliCat with her. Alex agreed, telling her they'd install a cat door in the kitchen door.

As soon as she pulled up to the house and opened the door to her car, CaliCat jumped off her lap and ran off. "Oh, Cali," she called after her, "you silly little cat. You're going to love it here!"

Rose spent the remainder of the day walking in and out of the kitchen, looking through the design magazines, talking with Heidi and Chloe, and finally making some decisions. Work had already begun on the infrastructure. Robby, the contractor whom Alex had known for many years, had hired subcontractors for the wiring and the plumbing. Once these jobs were completed, the heating and air conditioning would be installed.

Rose and Alex had committed to use turquoise, blues, greens, orange and gold throughout the bottom level of the house. Colored kitchen appliances were all the rage, and she decided they would buy all new appliances in the trendy new avocado green color. The walls would be white, and she was certain she could find an avocado and turquoise print for the curtains by the kitchen table. The barstools she would buy to sit at the island would have cushions on them, probably in a solid or print turquoise. In addition to the recessed lighting that would be installed, she would hang one large pendant over the island to provide special illumination for Heidi and Chloe's cooking. And despite Alex's distaste for anything hippy, she would hang several pots of various herbs. It wasn't hippy; it was gourmet. She was eager to get out to her studio and create an artist's rendition of her design. But it was late so that would have to wait until tomorrow or the next day.

"What did you come up with," asked Alex when he came up to the bedroom, which she now shared with him.

"I think you're going to love it. But instead of explaining, I'm going to paint a rendition of it. You'll get a better idea if you have a visual creation to see."

He came up to her and took her in his arms. "I'd like to see this visual creation," he cooed as he began to unbutton her blouse. He took his time undressing her until she had nothing on, not even her bra or panties. But he never got undressed. They spent the next hour in bed, touching and feeling and moaning, Rose completely nude and he still in his clothes, an entirely new sensation for her. Rose unbuttoned his Levis and crawled on top of him and began to rock rhythmically, his manhood inside her. When they had both climaxed, she lay down next to him, both of them on their backs looking up at the ceiling.

"You sure know how to please a man, Rose."

"I'm not really all that experienced, Alex. I don't want you to think I've been promiscuous, because I haven't.

"I'm not interested in your sexual history, and I'm not going to share mine with you. We have each other now, and you make me very happy."

"You are like no man I've ever been with. When I'm with you, well, you put me into another dimension. I'm completely yours, under your spell. I've never felt like this before."

"It's love. Loving the person you're with makes all the difference, honey."

They got up and got into the shower together, where they lathered each other up and shared a mutual orgasm. As Rose was drying off, she asked, "Alex, why don't you have any window dressing over that large window?" The huge bathtub sat right under the window.

"It's never had one, as far as I know. No one's ever out there. The orchards and cattle ranch are in the back of the house, except for the acreage that spreads out to the north and south, which are some distance away. Besides, that window faces west. The only people who would ever be out there are people who would be coming up to the front door, and most of them I'd be expecting. You'll have to try out that bathtub. It's quite an experience," he added as he gave her a friendly squeeze on her buttock.

By the time they got back downstairs, the girls were setting the meal on the table.

Chapter 13

April 4
*Martin Luther King, Jr., in Memphis for the sanitation
workers' strike, is fatally shot on the balcony of the
Lorraine Motel.   Gunman James Earl Ray, a white
supremacist, flees the country. Over the next week, riots
in more than 100 cities nationwide leave 39 people dead,
more than 2,600 injured and 21,000 arrested.*

"I don't know what to say to him," complained Rose.
They were on their way to Riverside to meet with Mr.
Novak, the criminal defense attorney recommended by
Alex's personal attorney.

"I think all you're going to do today is answer
questions. Be honest. Don't hide anything. If you'd like
me to sit in the outer office while you talk to him, I will."

"No, I want you with me. You already know every shameful detail."

They walked into the building and were shown to Mr. Novak's office. Shortly after they sat down in the waiting area, his secretary informed them that Mr. Novak would see them now. Alex accompanied Rose into his office, where the attorney offered them each a seat across from his large desk.

"You don't look like a felon," the attorney said, breaking the ice and getting a little laugh out of all of them.

"I did something really stupid," offered Rose.

"I got the police report and the pictures that were taken inside the house. You aren't holding a marijuana cigarette in any of the pictures. That's good. They can't really prove possession, unless they're going to claim that the close environment presupposed possession. We're not going to worry about the charge for selling the drug. You bought it, you didn't sell it. I'm afraid the same can't be said for your friend Kyle. He's going to have a hard time getting out of this. He's probably looking a few years prison time."

That hit Rose like a ton of bricks. She looked at Alex for some comfort, but he just raised his eyebrows as if to say, "What'd you expect?"

"You have a hearing set for July. I'm hoping I can get the whole thing thrown out."

"Thrown out? How could that be? I thought I was going to prison."

"There's always that possibility. What you did was extremely foolish, but they don't have any real evidence against you. I couldn't find any past arrests on you. If there are any, you need to let me know now."

"No! I mean, no sir. I've never been arrested before."

"Do you have a continuous work record?"

"No. I've never really had to work. My family set up a trust fund. But I do work if I find something interesting, like the MacKenzie Local Hist…"

"Another trust fund baby. Find something to convince the court that you're a contributing member of society. Before July."

"I will. I promise, Mr. Novak."

They left the attorney's office and went to D'Elia's for pastrami sandwiches. As usual, Rose only took a few bites of hers, so Alex ate hers after he had finished his own.

After lunch, they went to some fabric shops to look at material for the kitchen curtains and barstools. They found several they liked but, didn't buy anything just then. She still wasn't certain about what she wanted to do with the windows.

The old Ford truck didn't have a radio in it, so they were unaware of the news that rocked the country, until they got home and Alex turned on the 6:00 news. Martin Luther King, Jr. had been shot, fatally. Rose stood in front of the TV, frozen. Heidi and Chloe came out and stood with her, until they all sat down at once on the sofa in front of the television.

They all had sandwiches for dinner that night. Rose drank too much wine and went to bed, feelings of despair and shame trailing up the stairs with her.

The next day Rose took a transistor radio out to her studio, so she could listen to the uninterrupted broadcasts about Dr. King. She listened while she worked on the rendition of the kitchen. Riots had already started in cities around the country. *Ironic,* she thought. *His message was one of non-violence.*

Chapter 14

April 6
After a 90-minute shootout between Black Panthers and police in Oakland, California, police shoot Bobby Hutton, 17, as he tries to surrender.

Rose had never done interior design before and felt a bit overwhelmed by the coordination that had to be done. Alex had given her carte blanche in the kitchen. He even entrusted the appliances to her, telling her he had too much work to do on the ranch. Robby took measurements of the spaces for the refrigerator and oven range. Rose designated a spot near the sink where the dishwasher would go. This, of course, would require carpentry work, as old cupboards would need to be removed to make space for it. She was also getting a new sink, a big, two-sided one. This one would have a garbage disposal. Heidi and Chloe were beside themselves with excitement.

She set out in search of appliances. With the help of a very accommodating salesman, she purchased an avocado green side by side refrigerator, oven range, dishwasher, washer and dryer. The appliance store also sold small appliances, so she bought a turquoise blender, hand mixer, and even a turquoise vacuum cleaner. The salesman told her they would be available in about a week, but she told him he may have to hold on to them until the kitchen was ready for them. He gladly agreed.

The next week was a whirl of activity. The carpenter came and took out some bottom cupboards to make a space for the dishwasher. The electrician came and began replacing the existing lights with recessed lighting and installing the pendant light over the island. It hung low from the ceiling and looked like a large, turquoise, Japanese lantern.

The current washer and dryer were in an outdoor room. Rose decided that the new washer and dryer deserved a better environment. She had the carpenter tell her what could and couldn't be done in the space. They decided the space was large enough to accommodate a fairly large counter which could be used for folding clothes. A retractable indoor clothesline would be installed, as well as a fold-up ironing board. This area would be painted the same off-white as the kitchen, and the largest wall would be wallpapered in large turquoise and yellow sunflowers. She thought she might use this same wallpaper on one of the kitchen walls, over near the kitchen table, leading to the exit door.

As the work was coming together, Rose questioned the existing cupboards, which she noticed in the magazines were now referred to as cabinets. They were dark and heavy, and she was trying to give the place a lighter, airier look. She and Alex went into the kitchen and stood there, contemplating what Rose considered to be a problem, but what Alex had a hard time picturing. In the end, they decided to remove and discard all the cabinet doors, have the cabinets sanded and re-stained in a lighter blond, and have new doors made and stained to match. They would extend the top cabinets around to within inches of the big window in order to make up for the storage space they were losing because of the dishwasher. These corner cabinets would have lazy Susans on all shelves. Rose also decided that a few of the top cabinets would have glass doors. Thinking about that, she realized she would need to buy all new dinnerware, so the stacks of dishes, bowls, cups, and stemware would look nice behind the glass doors.

She had also decided not to have a curtain over the sink. With the new cabinets coming within inches of the window, she thought it better to install a woven wood Roman shade. She chose an off-white to match the paint on the walls.

There was a dinette area just beyond the kitchen, that led to a door to the garden. She ultimately decided against using a curtain on the dinette window; the window there would get the same woven wood treatment as the one above the sink. The wall across from the window would be wallpapered in the same paper that would be used in the laundry room.

Rose ultimately chose a large round white Formica dinette table. Around the table were four swivel Eames club chairs with chrome bases and casters. These were upholstered in bright-yellow Naugahyde. Rose thought the chairs would offer both comfort and utility and would brighten up a space already dominated by avocado green and turquoise. Plus, they matched the sunflowers in the wallpaper. Over the table hung a "Sputnik" sphere chandelier, reflecting the current race to space and bringing the kitchen into the mid-20th century.

The original flooring, which was by now about 100 years old, was made of dark, wide planks. Rose thought they could be sanded down to their natural color and stained a lighter color to match the cabinets. But if they did the kitchen, they would need to do the living room, dining room, and the two offices downstairs. Then of course the stairway would look odd if they didn't sand and re-stain it as well. But then they'd have to do the upstairs walkway in front of the front-facing guest rooms. Would it then look funny to leave the guest rooms and Alex's room dark? Where would the project end? She decided against redoing any of the floors. She would brighten it up with area rugs.

Chloe answered the knock at the door. "Oh, hi Donna. Alex is upstairs. I'll go and get him." Rose came down the stairs with Alex. She had no idea who Donna was when Chloe announced that she was here. Out of curiosity, she came down for a look. She saw an attractive woman about the same age as Alex.

Alex walked up to Donna and greeted her with a hug and kiss on the cheek. Donna asked, "Is that all? After all these months all I get is a hug?"

"Right. Well, uh, Donna, this is Rose."

Rose stood slightly behind Alex's right shoulder. She couldn't bring herself to say anything.

"Rose?" questioned Donna. "Hello Rose. It didn't take you long to move in on my territory, did it?"

"I don't know what you're talking about. Territory?"

"Yes, my territory. I left just before Thanksgiving to go to Oregon to help my father. He was ill. I didn't think I needed to worry about Alex waiting for me."

"Rose, would you excuse us for a minute? Donna and I need to talk."

Rose retreated upstairs. Shortly, Alex came up. "That was awkward."

"And unexpected," replied Rose. "Could you explain?"

"I used to see her." He paused, and Rose didn't say anything. "OK, it was more than that. But it was never really serious." Another pause. "OK, it was serious."

"Do you love her?"

"No. I guess I never did."

"But she seems to think you did. How long did it go on?"

"I don't know."

"Months? Longer?

"Several years."

"Well no wonder she thought you would wait! Alex, you were in a committed relationship! Why didn't you tell me?"

"I never felt that committed. It was comfortable. The time just went by."

"She's attractive. She seemed very confident in herself."

"She's a commercial realtor. She owns her own business. She's very successful."

Rose felt small. What did she have to compare to this woman? Donna was successful and obviously very competent. "Would you like me to leave?"

"What? No! Rose, it's over. She's gone."

"Alex, a woman shows up at your door, expecting to start up where she left off. You've never mentioned a word about her to me. She's pretty, she's successful, and she thought she was yours. If that's what you want, tell me. I'd rather hear it now than later."

"I've told you Rose. I love you. I've never loved anyone else. Not Donna, not anyone." He pulled her close to him and held her. Finally, he gave her a soft kiss. "It's over. I want you."

The Porsche pulled off the road and Rose took a look at the map. The carpet store was supposed to be on this block, but she didn't see it anywhere. She pulled her car into the parking lot of a place called "Shepherd Ministries" to ask for help. She had no idea what kind of a business this was. There were people lounging around the steps as she walked up and went inside. She entered a lobby, where a woman behind a glass window asked if she could be of assistance. Rose gave her the address she was looking for and the lady immediately spotted the problem. "You're looking for East Arlington, Ma'am. This is West Arlington."

"Oh, I see."

"Just keep driving a few miles east. You'll find it."

"Thank you so much. By the way, what kind of a business is Shepherd Ministries?"

"We're a halfway house, Ma'am. We cater to people who are recently out of prison or recovery programs. We shepherd them back to independence. Most of these people have been drug or alcohol users, and as I said, some of them are just out of prison. They need support, and that's what we give them."

"I see," but she wasn't really sure what they did for these people. "Are they all men?"

"No, we take in females too. Although right now we only have one woman in residence."

"OK. Well, thank you." She turned to leave and get on with her purpose of finding the carpet store. But something, she couldn't articulate what, made her stop and turn back around. She walked back up to the window. "Do you have any opportunities for volunteer work?"

"Oh goodness yes. Pastor Hartgrove manages the volunteers, and just about everything else," she laughed. "He might be available. Would you like to talk to him?"

"Yes, yes I think I would."

Pastor Hartgrove came out to greet Rose and escort her back to his office, which was sparsely furnished. A big picture of Jesus hung over his desk. A dead plant hung in the corner. The desk was made of dinged-up metal that looked like it was probably an

Army issue. The chairs were heavy, also made of metal with seats made of brown Naugahyde padding that had stuffing breaking through the cracks in them. Rose hesitantly sat down in one.

"So, Mrs. Green tells me you're interested in volunteering here at Shepherd Ministries?"

"Yes. Anyway, I'd like to talk about it."

"OK. We always need help with the housekeeping chores. And the soup lines. We serve everyday beginning at 7:00 A.M. for two hours and again at 5:00 P.M., also for two hours. If you're interested in helping us to transport our residents you'll need a California Driver's License with a passenger endorsement. Do any of these opportunities interest you?"

Rose felt like she had entered another dimension. "Well, uh, I was actually thinking more about offering an art class."

"An art class? Oh, my goodness. We did have a group come in one time and teach our residents how to fill out job applications. That was much appreciated, but they only came a few times and that was that. An art class, you say?"

" 'I am seeking. I am striving. I am in it with all my heart.' Vincent Van Gogh said that. It sounds to me that many of your residents could relate to that, Pastor."

"We don't have funding for materials, Miss Lefebre."

"I can bring them. All I'll need is a space. We could even work outdoors if we had too, provided it's not raining."

"I'm willing to give it a try. When might you like to begin?"

"I'm not sure. I'll have to talk it over at home, and see what might be a good day that I could come in. I'm thinking about coming in once a week. I could probably start in a couple of weeks."

Pastor Hartgrove wrote out his phone number on a piece of paper. "And we have an activity room. I think you could set up in there."

"Thank you, Pastor. I'll call you." Rose walked out to her car like she was walking on air. She couldn't explain why.

A halfway house? No way am I going to let you work at a halfway house!" Rose had never heard Alex raise his voice before.

"I don't need your permission, Alex," she retorted.

"Do you have any idea what kind of people hang around those places, Rose?"

"Yes, I do. Former addicts, alcoholics, and prisoners. Emphasis on former!" She stressed the word. "And I'm not going to be alone. There's a staff that works there. I'll go during the day. I'll be fine."

"What in the hell gave you the idea to do that?"

Rose explained to him how she had gotten lost looking for the carpet store and had pulled up to the place to ask directions. "What gave me the idea? I honestly don't know. I just felt compelled to do it. I still do." CaliCat jumped into her lap, somehow knowing that she needed comforting.

"I'm not going to be able to go with you and sit with you, Rose. I've got too much to do around here."

"I don't expect you to. Look, I'll go once and if it doesn't work out I won't go back. I do want to be safe, you know. Unlike you, I think I will be. I'm not worried about it."

Alex changed the subject. "I was talking to the carpenter today and he thinks we should have the house treated for termites."

"Termites? Is there a problem?

"Not bad. He says he's actually impressed that there's so little damage. But the house is almost 100 years old. I think he's right. We need to have it tented and we'll have to move out for several days. I thought we could go to your place.

Chapter 15

April 11
Johnson signs the Fair Housing Act, banning discrimination in housing on the basis of race, color, religion, or national origin. It is the last of the landmark civil rights laws he signed.

Laguna Beach had been an artists' colony since the first decade of the century, ever since Plein Air artists like William Wendt and California marine artist Frank Cuprien moved to the area. Within a few years, Laguna Beach had a permanent population of about 300 people, half of whom were artists. By the 1920s, summer cottages dotted the landscape.

In 1932 the **Festival of Arts** staged its first show in the downtown area, hoping to draw some additional business to town after the Los Angeles Olympic Games. A local artist added 'living pictures' to the festival, launching the tradition of the **Pageant of the Masters.**

The city had already caught the eye of Hollywood filmmakers. Hollywood stars like Bette Davis, Mary Pickford, Judy Garland, Rudolph Valentino, Charlie Chaplin and Mickey Rooney maintained homes in town.

Now, in the '60s, the city was home to a growing population of hippies. Alex didn't hide his disdain from them, reminding Rose often that they needed to get a job or join the military. But the city had so many galleries and eateries that he couldn't deny its attraction. And, of course, there was the beach, that beautiful blue ocean that stretched beyond the horizon.

They sat on Rose's porch, high on a cliff where they had an expansive view of the ocean. Sailboats were sailing by, and in the distance they could see an oil tanker heading north, probably to the Los Angeles harbor, where the crude oil would be transported to Wilmington to be refined. Rose was drinking a glass of chilled white wine and Alex was drinking Scotch, neat. CaliCat was settled comfortably on Rose's lap. She glared at Alex. When he put his arm around Rose, Cali hissed at him.

As the sun dipped below the horizon and the air began to cool, Rose said, "Let's go in the hot tub."

"OK, but no dope."

"Of course not, Alex! I told you, I'm done with all that."

"I know you are, honey. I was just confirming that." He kissed her briefly. "I've never been in a hot tub before."

"Then you're in for a treat!"

They went inside, stripped, got some towels and headed out the back door. Alex stopped to refresh their drinks before he went out, and by the time he got to the hot tub Rose was already submersed in it. The jets were humming, creating a circulating eddy of aerated temptation. He dropped his towel and climbed in. As he was lowering himself onto the bench, Rose said, "You're body is so tan, but your legs are white."

"If you want, I can take off my pants while I work with the horses." This elicited laughter from both of them. "Hey, this is nice. We might have to get one of these at the ranch."

"In some of the magazines I've been going through, I notice they're building them right in to the side of swimming pools. You said you want to put in a new pool. Maybe you should do that!" They sat on the bench that ran the perimeter of the redwood tub, facing each other, while they sipped their drinks.

Rose set her wine glass on the rim of the tub and moved toward Alex on her knees. He set his Scotch on the rim and leaned into her. The kiss started out gentle and then became possessive. Rose could feel the bubbles from the jets swirling around her most sensitive area.

She moaned. Alex kissed her nipples, licked them, and gently bit them. "Let's go into the bedroom," she suggested.

In the bedroom they dropped their towels to the floor and slid into the waterbed. They kissed, possessive, demanding kisses. Rose crawled on top of him and kissed his chest while her fingers found their way to the course hair below the line of dark hair that led from his chest to below his navel. His member was hard. She began to massage it, first gently and then harder and faster. Her finger felt the tip of it and she swirled her finger over the seminal fluid. Alex was moaning. She lowered herself onto his member and sat up. Moving up and down with the tide of the waterbed, she could feel him moving in and out of her. He was large and hard, and she could feel every inch of him rubbing against her erogenous zone. They climaxed together, and she collapsed on top of him. Alex held her and rubbed his hands gently up and down her back. "Can we do this every night for the rest of our lives?" he asked.

Alex was awakened when Rose brought in a tray with coffee and toast on it. She opened the curtains and let the morning sun infuse the room with light. "You're going to make a spoiled man out of me, Rose."

Rose laughed. "I don't ever see that happening," she responded. CaliCat was on the bed near Alex's feet. He dared not move them out of fear of repercussions. But Rose sat on the edge of the bed and scooped the cat into her arms, where the cat purred and positioned her head for maximum head scratching.

"What time is it anyway," asked Alex.

"After 9:00."

"What? After 9:00? I haven't slept in this late since I was a teenager! I wonder what happened to me."

"Could it have been the four glasses of Scotch, the hot tub, good sex, and a waterbed?" They both laughed.

"What are we going to do today?" he inquired.

"I'd like to take a walk on the beach. It's a gorgeous spring day."

"Sounds good. I'll need a couple more cups of coffee, a quick shower, and I'll be good to go."

It was a Sunday, and there were a lot of people on the beach. Some were lying on towels or blankets sunning themselves, talking, and reading. Others were in the water, attempting to body surf in the shallow, soupy, water. Some were simply playing in the sand where the waves washed up on shore, trying to run ahead of the wave before it caught them. Many, like Rose and Alex, were simply walking along the tide line and enjoying the atmosphere.

"What do you want out of life, Rose?"

"I want what most women want. I want to get married and have children. I want a husband who loves me and can provide for me."

"I'm not sure that's what most women want anymore. You're an old-fashioned girl, I guess." He put his arm around her and they slowed their pace.

"I guess at heart I am. But I also want to continue my art. I don't want to give that up. What do you want?"

"A woman to love. One who loves me. A woman who will be home when I come in late from work. A woman who's not afraid to have a good time in bed." Here they both laughed, thinking of last night. He took his arm off her shoulder and took her hand, and they continued walking.

They had walked a long distance along the shore, at least two miles, then back the same distance. As it was nearing 1:00, Alex suggested they get something to eat. There was a lovely seafood restaurant on the strand, and they decided to eat there. Rose ordered a bowl of cioppino and a glass of white wine. Alex ordered a seafood platter and a beer.

When they got back to the house, Alex sat back with the newspaper and another beer. Rose continued reading the journals. Someone knocked at the door. Rose got up to answer it and found Kyle standing on her porch. "Oh, hi Kyle." She had intended to tell him she had company and couldn't visit with him, but before she had a chance to say anything, he walked right past her into her living room.

Alex stood up. "How are you doing, Kyle?"

"Huh. I didn't expect to see you here."

"Oh, I'm here alright."

"I need to talk to Rose."

"Go ahead. Don't let me stop you."

"In private."

Rose cut in. "Kyle, Alex knows everything. You can talk to me here. Why don't you have a seat?" Kyle sat down. "I talked to a public defender. So did some of the others. Want me to give you his name?"

"No, thank you. I have my own attorney."

"Probably the best money can buy, huh?" Rose didn't respond to this remark. "The proletariat has to rely on the county's PD." He looked at Alex for a challenge to his statement, but Alex didn't say anything. "Anyway, he thinks he might be able to get some of the charges reduced."

"That's good, Kyle. I'm glad to hear that," offered Rose.

"What about you?"

"Well, we went to talk to an attorney, but we haven't heard back from him yet." That was as much as she was willing to tell him for now.

"Yeah, well, my guy said he might be able to get some of the charges reduced," emphasizing the "might" and the "some." "That's not good enough for me. I'm still looking at two felonies. He even said I'm probably going to have to do some time."

"Kyle, I don't know what to say. Maybe he'll get them reduced to misdemeanors."

Kyle laughed, a sarcastic, derisive laugh. "That's the thing with these PDs. They ain't gonna do shit for us. Their caseloads are so overbooked they just take the easiest way out. What's it to him if I do time? He doesn't give jack shit."

Alex interrupted, "Kyle, please don't curse like that in front of Rose."

"Rose? Like she's some kind of a fragile petal? I can assure you she's not!"

In less than two seconds Alex was out of his seat, had yanked Kyle up by his t-shirt, and was standing inches from Kyle's face. "You apologize to Rose right now, or you're going to find yourself sprawled out on the sidewalk."

"Oh God. Sorry. I didn't want it to go like this. I actually wanted to ask for your help, Rose."

"My help?" asked Rose. "How could I help you, Kyle?"

"I need a real lawyer. A good one. I know you can help me, Rose."

Rose stared at him for a few seconds, dumbstruck, then glanced at Alex. Alex surreptitiously shook his head from side to side, almost unnoticeable. But Rose got the message. She wasn't sure how to respond to Kyle, so Alex answered for her. "Rose can't do that, Kyle. You each got yourselves into this, and you're each going to have to get yourselves out of it."

"Should I have expected anything less of the bourgeoisie? Go fuck yourselves." Alex got one good punch in before Kyle stumbled out the door and left.

Rose was shaking. Alex put his arm around her and led her back to the sofa. Then she started crying. "I don't know what was more appalling," she got out in between sniffles, "his anger or your violence."

"How about his appalling nerve to come here and ask you to pay for a lawyer for him?"

"Alex, what he said about me. I, I..."

"Rose, we don't need to talk about that. You owe me no explanation. I told you before I don't want to know anything about your past sexual experiences, and I'm not going to share mine with you. We're together now, we move on from here."

"But, it's important to me that you know I haven't been promiscuous."

"I didn't think you were. Come here, my little bourgeoisie princess." He took her in his arms. "I'm sorry I was violent. It's too bad he fell out the door. I had a lot more planned for him." He lifted her head and gently kissed her lips. "I'm sorry I upset you."

Chapter 16

April 23

*Students take over five buildings on Columbia
University's campus and briefly hold a dean hostage,
calling for the university to cut its ties to military
research. Before dawn on April 30 administrators call
in the police, who respond with about 1,000 officers.
More than 700 people are arrested, and 132 students,
four faculty and 12 officers are injured.*

Ooooh, what do you think of this?" Rose asked Alex as
she held up a bolt of satin fabric with dark green, gold,
white, and orange stripes on it. They had been back from
Laguna for several days. The workmen were just about
finished in the kitchen, and work was beginning in the
living room. They had agreed to carry the green from

the kitchen into the living room and bring in gold and orange. Rose loved the natural elements of the house: the wood, the plastered walls, high beam ceilings, and the large windows that allowed the outdoors to become a part of the room. The room would be done mostly in greens and gold, but would include orange as a complementing color, which would also tie the room to the outdoors, where one could see the orange groves in the distance.

"I like it," answered Alex, not really sure of how the room would eventually look, but definitely sure he shouldn't question Rose about the decorating. So far, she had proven herself to be talented and tasteful, and he was certain he would like the finished product. Rose suggested that the two upholstered chairs, one on either end of the long sectional they were getting, be upholstered in the same satin stripe as the drapes.

Two Eames lounge chairs and ottomans would be placed in the alcove beneath the large, west-facing window. Rose had chosen these for the beautiful wooden base of the chair that she thought would complement the flooring, which had been a timeless feature of the house since it had been built 100 years ago. Also, the leather was available in a dark olive green, which complemented the avocado green in the kitchen, which could be seen from this intimate conversation place. She planned to throw a couple of pillows on each of the chairs that would tie in the colors from the rest of the room. An Aubusson rug defined the space and brought in all the colors of the room, which added to the décor of the house: reds, oranges, yellows, turquoise and greens were muted on an ivory background. A large vase of fresh flowers would always be placed on the round table between the chairs. She knew this would require a standing order of flowers to be delivered weekly by a local florist. The more she thought about it, she would place fresh flowers all around the house, and all of them would be delivered weekly.

The day after they bought the chairs, they went out again in search of a sectional. Rose wanted a long, low sectional with tapered wooden legs. They found a sample that could be custom made to their specifications. It would be placed in the center of the room, facing the fireplace. Rose considered herself fortunate that the huge fireplace was finished with large beautiful river rocks that would complement the new décor. The sectional had to be long because the room was so large. The main length of the sofa would be nine feet. Forming a round corner on one side would be a five-foot section and rounding out the other side would be a three-foot section. The entire sofa would be covered in gold fabric, with matching gold stitching giving it a formal, quilted look on the backs and seat cushions. Alex suggested they could have it covered in plastic, that he knew someone who had covered all their furniture and it kept it from wear and tear. Rose stared at him and then said, "No." They bought two chairs in the same design, but Rose told the salesman to hold off on the upholstery until she found what she wanted. And now she had. A room-size area rug, in a plush silk the same color as the sectional, would define the living area.

Alex proclaimed he was done shopping for furniture, so Rose assured him that she would finish up from there; that is, until it was time to do the bedroom.

Chapter 17

April 29, 1968
*Hair opens on Broadway and runs for more than 1,700
performances, introducing mainstream theatergoers to
sex, drugs, rock 'n' roll and draft resistance.*

That probably would have been Dede," Alex said. Rose
was getting ready to read Carolina de Silva's, her great-
grandmother's, memoir, and she told Alex that her
mother had mentioned that Carolina knew his father and
mother.

"Oh," she answered. "My mother and I assumed
it was your parents."

"I don't know. My parents didn't go out much.
My dad was getting old and my mom wasn't much of a

social butterfly. But read it and let me know." Once again, that fleeting but guilty thought went through his mind. *Why did my father marry my mother? What did he see in her?*

"Isn't it amazing that our families' lives crossed way back then? Almost a hundred years ago! Alex, I can't wait until you meet my mother. You're going to love her and she's going to love you!"

"If she's anything like you then I know I'll love her."

"Oh but she's not! She's good and kind and just the loveliest person you'll ever meet!"

"Well you're good and kind and lovely."

"Not like her. She's so sophisticated and poised. She could have been a professional ballerina. But she told me that by the time it was ready for her to go off to continue her training she was kind of tired of ballet. She'd been doing it all her life. She opted to go to college instead."

"Sounds like her grandmother did a good job raising her. I'm looking forward to hearing about her memoirs."

Rose had her hands full with her studio, decorating, and reading the journals and memoir. But she still yearned to set up a schedule for teaching art classes at the half-way house, so she called Pastor Hartgrove. They settled on Tuesday mornings at 10:00. Today was the first class.

She arrived early and carried in her supplies: easel, paper, acrylic paints, brushes, table-top easels and pre-stretched canvasses. She would use the large easel to model the lesson, one step at a time. The students would sit at tables in the multi-purpose room with their canvasses on the smaller easels and follow her instructions. In this first lesson she would show them how to draw a bicycle with a basket of flowers attached to the handlebars.

She had no idea how many students would show up. It turned out there were three of them, one woman and two men. She wasn't sure what she was expecting, but she was glad to see that they were all clean and wearing clothes that looked freshly laundered. Years of hard living showed in all their faces. The silence among them created an awkward rift between them and her.

First, she painted the frame of the bicycle, one stroke at a time, the students imitating her every stroke. As she painted, she talked, and before long the three students loosened up and began to chatter among themselves and with her. She didn't learn anything about their lives or their past troubles, but she did learn that the woman, Pamela, had a lot of potential for art.

"They were so nice, Alex!" she reported enthusiastically when she got home. "They genuinely seemed to like the lesson! And we talked and laughed and had fun. I was afraid it was going to be dark and awkward, but it wasn't. It was fun!"

"I'm glad to hear that, honey. I'm still not happy about you spending time at a half-way house."

"Oh don't be so silly. The pastor is there, and the secretary, and other staff members. I don't think these people are dangerous, Alex. They've just been down and out."

"Because of their own decisions," countered Alex.

"Probably. But not everyone has had the support and resources that we've had. As they say, 'There but for the grace of God go I.'"

"That's one of the reasons I love you Rose. You're a good person."

The next week the same three students showed up, and this time there were four more. Rose had decided to teach a still life lesson for this week's class. She brought in a large cardboard box to elevate the items they'd be drawing and placed a cloth over the box to disguise it, making it look more like a table than a box. On top of it she placed a fishing tackle box, a creel, and a reel. She thought this subject might appeal more to the men in the class than a lesson drawing flowers or butterflies, although those would have been easier.

Pamela was still the only woman in the class. As the lesson progressed, the students once again engaged in friendly chatter. She learned the backgrounds of some of them. Several of them were alcoholics, now in recovery. One man, Earl, had been arrested for driving under the influence and had served two years in jail. Pamela had been arrested for writing checks from someone else's account and had recently been released after three years in jail. She was in her early 40s but looked older. She told the group she had been living on the streets and had no money for food. She stole a checkbook out of a stranger's purse and attempted to write a check for cash. She had been desperate, and she paid the price for it. Rose thought about what Alex had said about making bad decisions, and she supposed he was right. She had no idea how Pamela had ended up living on the street, or why she couldn't rely on family or friends for support. Her own bad decisions, probably, and bad behavior. Still, Rose felt sorry for her. More than that, she liked her.

Driving home that day, Rose thought about her own bad decision to smoke pot and considered the fact that she and Pamela weren't so different after all.

Thinking about that made her wonder what was happening with her own case.

It was 3:00 in the afternoon when Mr. Novak, the attorney, called. Alex was home working in his office that day, so they both listened in to the telephone receiver. Stunned, Rose asked, "You mean it's over?"

"It's over," Mr. Novak assured her. "They dropped all charges against you. They just didn't have enough evidence to pursue your case."

"What about the hearing in July?"

"No need. There is no case."

"What about the others, my friends?"

"I don't really have any information about them. I'm sure some of them will be prosecuted. Especially that Kyle character. I suspect he's going to do some time."

The call ended. "Hey, why do you look so sad? You should be ecstatic! You're in the clear!" said Alex.

"I am. But Kyle isn't. I feel guilty that I'm off scot free and he's probably going to jail."

"Kyle made his bed, Rose. He had dope parties and accepted money for the dope. And he's a commie. If it hadn't been this it would be something else in the near future. Don't you dare feel guilty about him. He's an asshole."

But Rose did feel guilty. And she felt sorry for him. But she also knew she couldn't do anything to help him. Alex was right about one thing; he had made his own bed.

Rose had set Dede's journals aside while she indulged herself in her great-grandmother's memoir. What an amazing woman she was! She had come from Peru, the daughter of wealthy parents, but found herself stranded in America. She managed to become one of the wealthiest landowners in Orange County. She counted people like the Yorbas and the Irvines among her friends. Like Alex's father, Carolina de Silva and her husband planted orange groves. It was a time when California was booming, enticing people to move west with the lure of oranges. Rose read about Carolina and her first husband, who had built the house she herself had been raised in, and where her own parents still lived. She read about their daughter, who was her own mother's mother. Her mother never spoke much about her mother, and now she was learning why. She barely knew her. The mother, whose name was Marguerite but who was called Margie, was a real piece of work. She was mostly absent in Edna's life, but she would breeze in and stir up havoc whenever she was there. That's why her mother's grandmother, Carolina, raised her. Reading the memoir, Rose realized that her mother's sophistication, elegance, and poise came from Carolina.

Now she was reading about Carolina's second husband. It was he who was a friend of Alex's father, and it was indeed Dede whom her great-grandmother had met. Rose pondered what it must have been like to be in the presence of these two dynamic, successful, beautiful women. Talk about role models! She decided to put the memoir down for now and get back to reading Dede's journals, to see if Dede had mentioned Carolina. It would be fun to read the journals and the memoir together from that point on, chronologically following these women through the years.

There was something else about these women, Dede, her great-grandmother, and her own mother. They were all very devout Catholics. She started thinking that maybe she would start going to church more regularly. Right now, she only went when she spent a weekend at her parents' house.

Then she began to wonder about Alex's mother. Her name was Carole. Alex didn't talk much about her, although she knew he loved her. She needed to find out more about this woman who married Dede's widower. She had certainly raised a wonderful son!

Chapter 18

May 17

Nine antiwar activists enter a Selective Service office in Catonsville, Maryland, remove nearly 400 files and burn them in the parking lot with homemade napalm. The example of the Catonsville Nine (later convicted of destruction of government property and sentenced to jail terms between 24 and 42 months) spurs some 300 similar raids on draft boards over the next four years.

The living room paint was nearing completion. Before work had begun on the living room, Alex had made the decision to have all the windows in the entire house replaced. This huge project began in the living room, then to the kitchen, where touchups had to be made to the paint that had already been used in there. Now the workmen had moved upstairs, as every window in all nineteen rooms would be replaced. All the new windows were double-paned, a design which had been introduced in the last decade. Alex claimed these windows would keep the house cooler in the summer and warmer in the winter.

"Why are you staring at me?" asked Rose.

"Whatever became of you modeling for Andy Warhol?" he answered with a handsome grin.

"I wasn't going to model. I was going to be in one of his short films. I suspect he's forgotten all about me."

"Good." Rose knew he was being playful, and she marveled at how much she had changed in the five months since she had met Alex. If Mr. Warhol called her tomorrow, she didn't think she'd even take him up on his offer. Well, maybe she would. But she knew it was a moot point, because he wasn't about to call.

The art classes at the half-way house continued. There were twenty people in residence, and Rose had a steady class of about a dozen students every week. Many of the residents had jobs and could not attend the classes. She currently had them involved in a multi-step process of making macraméd plant holders with pots they had made themselves. One week she taught them how to make coil pots. The next week, when she picked up the dried clay pots to take them home to put in her kiln, they started on the macraméd holders. They all made good progress with their macramé, but they had to finish them on their own, because it was too big a project to be done in one sitting. The third week they glazed the bisque pots, which she then took back to put in the kiln again.

Today, they would be planting a plant in the pot, and arranging the pot in the hanger. Rose had been to a nursery and had bought a variety of indoor plants. The students could choose from coleus, philodendron, spider plants, sword ferns, asparagus ferns, English ivy, or schefflera. The time was taken up with potting and arranging, and in the end, everyone was more than pleased with their product. Rose picked up the one remaining plant, a philodendron, and potted it in her own planter.

After the class was dismissed and she had cleaned up the room, she took her hanging plant and presented it to Pastor Hartgrove. "Here," she said, "it's time to replace that dead thing in your office." They both laughed, then the pastor told her how pleased he was with what she was doing. He added, "I guess there's a certain satisfaction people get from seeing a project through to completion, especially if you've put your own creativity into it."

"Yes, there definitely is. Pastor, are all of these students literate?"

"Literate? I think so. Why do you ask?"

"I'm thinking of expanding the classes to include a book discussion. You know, of certain artists or movements. I haven't really decided yet."

"I think that's a fine idea, Rose. Would everyone be reading the same book then?"

"Yes. I'll select one and buy multiple copies. And we'll continue with the art lessons, probably get back into acrylics."

"I hear the class has taken on a therapeutic aspect."

"They talk among themselves. I think it does them good. I stay out of it. I know nothing about psychology!"

"But you've given them a forum. We do have a group counselor in one evening a week. I'm glad the residents are opening up."

"It works both ways, Pastor. I'm learning a lot too."

Thy are the fairest maiden in the land, m'lady. Take this rose as a symbol of my love." Rose took the rose with the accompanying straight pin from the quasi-Shakespearean actor and fastened it to her white gauze blouse. She and her mother were at the Renaissance Pleasure Fair in Augora, about a two-hour drive from Riverside. They had been coming here every year for the past six years, since the first fair was held. Rose hadn't even bothered to ask Alex if he'd wanted to go; she knew he wouldn't. Besides, the event had become an annual tradition for her and Edna.

They walked through the booths, looking at the clothes, jewelry, leather, perfume, soaps, and other renaissance-era reproductions. Rose couldn't resist buying another peasant blouse, even though she already had several of them. Edna bought some French-milled soaps to have on hand for last-minute gifts. At a fine-arts booth, Rose bought some faux Fabergé eggs in colors that would match the new décor of Alex's house. She thought they might look pretty on the sideboard in the dining room.

"I sure like Alex."

"I love him, Mom. He's like no one I've ever met before."

"So you've told me. And that house! I've never seen anything like it!"

"Hah! It's such a mess with all the construction going on. You'll have to come back and see it when it's done."

Edna had driven to the ranch that morning and was going to spend the night so she wouldn't have to do too much traveling in one day. From the ranch, Rose drove her parents' Ford Galaxy to the fair, as she didn't think her mother would be too comfortable in the Porsche.

They stopped at a food booth where they each had a sandwich and enjoyed a small stein of beer.

"Oh, I haven't told you that I've been teaching an art class at a group home."

"You are? What kind of a group home?"

"It's a half-way house run by a small church. The residents are former alcoholics and addicts. Many of them are just out of jail or prison."

"Honey, that doesn't sound safe."

"Oh Mom. You sound like Alex. They're closely supervised, and the classes are in the multipurpose room, so there's staff around. I'm making a difference, Mom. The pastor says so and even I can see that it's making a difference in their lives." Rose went on to explain to her mother the different art projects she had taught them and what she had planned for the future.

"I'm proud of you, honey. My little girl is growing up."

"It's about time. Your little girl is 32." They both laughed.

Then they wandered over to watch an archery contest. On their way out they stopped at a booth that sold honey products, where Rose picked up some hand cream and soap for Heidi and Chloe. She also bought three jars of various kinds of honey.

When they got home, Edna went upstairs to lie down before dinner. But as she was hanging up her skirt and blouse in the wardrobe in the large guest room, her eye caught something on the bottom shelf. An envelope. It looked old. She opened the door and called out to Rose. "Rose, honey, can you come up here?"

When Rose entered the bedroom, Edna handed her the envelope saying, "Look what I found in the bottom of the wardrobe. It looks old."

They sat down together on the edge of the bed and opened it. It appeared to be written in the first person by someone named Carole. "Mom! It's from Alex's mother!"

"It looks like she wrote her own version of a memoir, however brief," replied Edna. "Do you think we should read it?"

"Let's." So together they read the 10 pages.

Carole

I never understood why Mac chose me. I was plain.
Not exciting. His first wife was beautiful and
apparently the star of the show wherever she went. And

highly educated, which I wasn't. I used to see them on the train to and from Los Angeles, because my daughter lived there, still does, actually, and they had several reasons to make the trip frequently. They made a striking couple. But a year after her death he boarded the train on the return to Riverside, walked to the back of the car, and sat down next to me. "I've seen you on this train before. Several times," he said.

"Yes, I've seen you too." He was even more handsome up close than he had been at a distance. He was wearing his hair shorter now than he had been the last time I saw him. It was gray, and he had it cropped close. "My name is Carole."

"Mac. Nice to finally meet you, Carole." He took a flask from his pocket and offered it to me. "Scotch?"

"No. No thank you." In those days I was a teetotaler, although years with Mac eventually brought me an appreciation of Scotch, and I enjoyed a glass of the oak-flavored spirit with him every night. I still do, even though I'm alone now.

"Can I get you anything? Coffee? Wine?"

"No, nothing, thank you."

He told me he had been in L.A. checking on their beach house, and to visit his wife's daughter and her children. He asked about my L.A. trips and I told him that my daughter lived there also. Eventually, he put his head back and fell asleep. When the train pulled into Colton, I was jarred awake to discover that I, too, had fallen asleep. What was really embarrassing was that my head had been resting on his shoulder! "Don't worry," he said, "I won't tell anyone."

"Tell anyone what?" I was offended at the insinuation that I had done something wrong.

"That we slept together." I was aghast, and I must have looked so because he added, "It's no big deal. We're both adults." Then he winked at me!

"Mr. MacKenzie, I resent your implication that..."

"Oh stop it. Can't you take a joke? Where are you going, anyway?"

"I'm transferring to Riverside, same as you."

"Then let me take you out to dinner when we get there. Allow me to make up for my rude sense of humor."

"You're forgiven. But I don't need to go out to dinner." But as I soon learned, what Mac wanted, Mac got. We went out to dinner and talked about the highlights of our life. He told me about losing Dede a year ago, about his ranch, his oil fields, and his two step-children. I told him my husband had died three years before. My daughter was married to a preacher and I was very proud of the life they were living. They were very involved with Aimee Semple MacPherson and the evangelist movement at her temple downtown. I could tell he wasn't impressed. His granddaughter, Maddie, was about the same age as my daughter. We talked until midnight, made plans to see each other

again, and that was the start of my life with Mac MacKenzie.

After a month he invited me to spend the weekend at his ranch. I was very hesitant, because I was sure I knew what he expected in return for his hospitality, and I wasn't sure how I would handle that. My husband and I had married very young, both very inexperienced, and our lovemaking never progressed beyond the basic ritual. I would let him climb on top of me, and I tolerated it while he put his organ inside of me. He would move and grunt and then get off me, leaving me with a creamy mess to clean up. I had been warned by my mother and a couple of ladies in our church, so I just considered it to be part of marriage. My God was I wrong!

The first night I spent with Mac was the beginning of a whole new world for me. He kissed me in a way I had never been kissed. I admitted to him that I didn't know much about the adult act. He looked up toward heaven and mouthed, "Thank you." I never understood why a man would thank God for giving him a middle-aged woman who knew nothing about making love.

Mac taught me everything there was about making love, anyway everything he wanted me to know about it. So many positions, terminology, things to do with different parts of your body, all sorts of things I had never known about but was eager to learn.

On the wall next to the bed were drawings of his wife in positions that left nothing to the imagination. She obviously knew a lot more about these acts than I did. It made me wonder about her. I had been told that she was very religious, a good person, but I had trouble reconciling that with the pictures on the wall. I grew up a strict Calvinist and was raised to believe that God punished people who engaged in behaviors such as Dede did. Of course, she had been a Catholic, and we Calvinists considered the Catholic Church to be a cult, full of false idolatry and wine drinking. I was told they worshiped the pope and saints and Christ's mother, but never prayed to God or read the Bible. Of course, I would soon learn that I had been misled. The next time I spent the night in Mac's luxurious bed the pictures were gone.

After we had been together for a while I asked if we could get a different bed. I was not comfortable making love to him in the bed he shared with Dede. We replaced it with a big, brass bed.

He shared with me how devastated he was when Dede died, but that he came to accept it soon after, an acceptance, he said, that was bestowed on him by her. She had suffered from severe rheumatoid arthritis, and in the years before her death she had been in a lot of constant pain. Mac thought this unending and excruciating pain had simply worn out her body. A few times I had seen him carrying her on or off the train. I felt bad that at the time I thought she was just being lazy, or silly, or I didn't know what. He told me that she loved to sew but hadn't been able to for a couple of years because her hands were so crippled. He came to accept that her death alleviated her pain, and he knew that she was in peace, living with her beloved God. He told me that it was she who directed him to me that day on the train. Even that, I felt, was her intrusion into our life.

A painted woman named Melody showed up at the house one afternoon. It turned out she had started coming around shortly after Dede died. She invited herself to stay for dinner and sat just to the left of Mac, who was at the head of the table. That was where I always sat, so I simply moved to sit at his right. Melody was about 10 years younger than me, but she had already been married and divorced twice. She dominated the conversation with a litany of complaints about her two former husbands. Then, she reached over and put her hand on top of Mac's. Looking at me in an attempt at coquettishness, she asked, "Did Mac tell you that he and I used to be lovers?"

"Melody, please!" admonished Mac. "That's inappropriate. Carole doesn't need to hear that."

"What? You never told her that we were engaged?"

"Melody, that was a long time ago, and we weren't actually ever engaged."

"Oh yes we were. Until that bitch came along and stole you away from me!"

Mac was out of his seat in a blink of an eye. He grabbed her by the upper arm and dragged her to the door, opened it, and shoved her out. That was the last I ever saw of that disagreeable woman. I have since wondered if he would have reacted the same if someone had said that about me.

Imagine my surprise when I found out I was expecting a child! I was afraid to tell him, afraid that he would be done with me. Why would a 66-year-old man want a baby? For that matter, why would a 46-year-old woman want one? But I was ecstatic, and as it turned out, so was Mac. We got married the next week. We married in the Catholic Church, for two reasons. One, I had already discovered they weren't as bad as I thought they were, and two, I didn't want to do anything that might give Mac cause to leave me.

When I moved into the house Mrs. Olsen, a surly woman whom I never really got to know, thank goodness, announced she was leaving. She had been with Mac for about 35 years, so I could see why she was ready to leave. Of course I knew that wasn't the real reason she was leaving. It was me. I guess she had loved Dede and couldn't accept a replacement. A lovely young woman named Ophelia took over as the head housekeeper, and Mac hired her sister, Callie, a girl of about fifteen, to help her.

Alex was born on November 4, 1920. Mac helped me to deliver, and though I was 46 years old, I had no problems. Alex and I were baptized into the Church on the same day in December of that year. My daughter was furious and threatened never to speak to me again. But of course she did.

When Alex was born, two young women came to stay at our house to help while I recovered. The first one was my daughter, Laura. The other one was Maddie. Maddie showed up with a girlfriend, Chloe, who would be with us for the first few days, but would then return to L.A. She and Maddie wore matching outfits of men's tuxedoes with white pleated shirts and patent leather shoes with white socks. They both had their hair bobbed and wore bright red lipstick. They stayed together in the same guest room. Laura declared that she would not stay under the same roof with them, which didn't help my recovery at all. Mac told her that Maddie loved to shock people, that she was genuinely a good person who really wanted to help me. In the end, Laura agreed to take a room that was as far away as she could get from the room Maddie and Chloe were sharing. Maddie was fun and gregarious. I never really got to know Chloe, as she was only there for a few days. But Laura was absolutely rude. Like me, she was raised to think all fun was sinful. She quoted the Old Testament about Sodom and Gomorrah, and the evils of man lying with man. Mac maintained there was nothing of the sort going on between Maddie and Chloe, that he knew something about homosexuality, and this wasn't it. The girls, he said, were wearing the latest fashion and acting in the current trend of androgyny. He was adamant that Maddie was not a homosexual.

Both Laura and Maddie were very helpful. They took turns getting up at night to walk and burp Alex after I had fed him. They promptly changed his diaper when he needed it. They took turns visiting with me as I recovered, which seemed a long time because of my age. But they had as little to do with each other as possible. Laura had to leave to get back to her family. Maddie stayed an extra week and, I have to admit, I really enjoyed having her around. As Alex grew, Maddie became his favorite relative. And through the years she proved herself to be a very loving and respectable woman.

I was 46 when Mac and I met on the train. He was 66, a full 20 years older than me, although his energy and personality made him seem younger than I, who was somber and quiet and dull. But through the years he taught me to have fun. He encouraged me to read, to learn about things that interested me, and we would have long talks when I would finish a book. Mac really brought out a new Carole, one that had been in me since I was a child, but who had faded into the background as I became a woman. I had been sober, dull, and judgmental. With Mac, I became happy, daring, fun, and yes, even passionate.

One afternoon a young man showed up at the ranch. He spoke in very broken English and introduced himself as Alexander. Mac stepped forward and gave him a big embrace, then stepped back and said, "Let me look at you, Alexander!"

"I'm good so far, Sir. That is, if I don't get the cancer."

"Alexander, you don't have to worry about that. If you would have been affected, it would have been shortly after you were born. You can quit thinking about that."

"Oh, that's a relief," he said in his new language. "Where is your wife who was with you? My father said she was very pretty. Is this your daughter?"

My eyes opened wide and then we all laughed. "No," answered Mac. "This is my wife. The lady your father met was my first wife. She passed away some years ago."

"Oh. Nice to meet you, second wife."

"Please, call me Carole."

It turned out that when Mac and Dede were in Greece, he delivered this young man! Unfortunately, the boy's mother died just after giving birth. The boy had only recently arrived in America to begin a new life. He was 20 years old.

Alex came in and was introduced to Alexander, beaming that he shared the same name. Mac commented that it was a hero's name, which I guess it was. Mac helped get Alexander a job on the docks at the Port of Los Angeles, where he is still working to this day. He and Alex have maintained a written correspondence, and Alex keeps me up to date on Alexander's life, his wife, and his three children. His wife, by the way, is a beautiful, red-headed Irish girl. Their kids are adorable.

When Alex was 10 Mac's health started to fail. He spent days writing a letter for me to give to Alex when he turned 18. In the letter, he assured Alex that he had been the love of his life, that he had brought meaning to his life, and that he loved me, his mother, for giving him a son. In addition to the Ten Commandments, he gave him 10 rules to live by.

1. *Enjoy life. Don't live your life in somber. There's a lot of fun to be had, so find it. And don't ever feel that you need to run this ranch. Do what makes you happy, but do something. Don't just live off your inheritance; that will not bring you happiness.*

2. *Travel. There's much to learn beyond your own city, state, and even country.*

3. *Dance. You'll have fun and you'll make the ladies happy.*

4. *Find one of the arts at which you can succeed. Paint, sing, play an instrument, any of the arts. It will make you a well-rounded person.*

5. *Attend a university. We have connections at Stanford, the University of Southern California, and the University of Riverside, but don't ever think you're limited to them. Go wherever you want to go, just be sure to graduate.*

6. *Study poetry. It will provide answers to life's questions. Memorize a few poems, the ladies are impressed with that. Shelley's To A Skylark is a good one.*

7. *Treat women with respect and be gentle with them. I know this from experience. I didn't*

always do this, but I've learned that when you do, they'll come back a hundred-fold and make you happy.

8. *Don't settle for just any woman. Find one who's fun, smart, and passionate. Beauty is a bonus.*

9. *Don't criticize people. If they need help, help them.*

10. *Don't fight someone else's war. War is brutal. War is ugly. War is hell.*

Mac died in 1930, shortly after the stock market crash, but the crash had nothing to do with it. He had been troubled all through 1928 and 1929 by the unprecedented climb of the stock values, and he knew the country was headed for trouble. He began to sell off his stocks, buying gold instead. He had the gold delivered to a warehouse he owned in town, to no one's knowledge. He and Alex, who was just a boy, went in at night and built a false wall to hide the gold. It was in the back behind pallets of toiletry products that a mother and daughter made out of oranges and lavender that grew on the ranch. Even they weren't aware of his and Alex's nighttime marauding. When the market crashed, we didn't lose a dime. Best of all, Alex got to work with his father on a clandestine operation known only to the three of us. They had a lot of fun doing that.

All of Mac's friends are gone now too. When Chet passed away Mary moved to live closer to her son, and the management of the estate was entrusted to Roderick, who had been working on the ranch since he

*was 14. He was one of Ophelia's many siblings who
had worked on and off, either at the ranch or in the oil
fields. Mac had sent Roderick to the University of
Riverside to study business, so he was very confident in
his ability to run all of his holdings. He is still
managing things for me. I don't know what I'd do
without him.*

When they were finished reading, they looked at
each other. "I don't think I would have liked her,
Mom."

"Oh, honey, don't say that. No woman would
have wanted to follow in Dede's footsteps. I'm sure she
was a very nice woman. Look at Alex!"

"I know, that's true. I need to find him and give
this to him." She left her mom to rest up and went to find
Alex. He was out in the groves, so she waited for him to
return to the house, then gave him the envelope,
admitting to him that she had already read it. He took it
into his office and closed the door.

As he read his mother's writing, tears welled up
in his eyes. He could sense her presence just as if she
were standing there beside him. His mother's feelings of
inferiority came through the pages quite obviously, and
he longed to hold her and remind her how much she was
loved. She had been such a good mother to him. What
was it now, fifteen years since she'd been gone? He felt
an overwhelming sense of loss.

He stayed in his office about an hour, then
emerged to find Rose in the living room watching *The*

Man from U.N.C.L.E. She turned it off when he sat down next to her. "You look sad," she said.

"Kind of, I guess. It was like having my mom here, talking to me. I miss her. She was a good mom."

"I'm sure she was. It was kind of sad, don't you think?"

"Yes. I always suspected she felt inferior to Dede. That came across quite clearly in these papers. But you know, my dad never treated her like that, at least that I could tell. Of course, I was only 10 when he died, so what would I know?"

"From what I gather from Dede's journals, your father was a wonderful, loving man, so I'm sure he did love her and treat her well."

"I don't know, Rose. Ever since I was a young man and I read Dede's journals, I've felt bad for my mother. She was the opposite of Dede. She was just a plain, ordinary woman. She wasn't dynamic. She was pretty, but not beautiful. She didn't really have any outstanding traits. Like I said, just an ordinary woman."

"Well your father must have found something extraordinary about her. He married her."

"That, and the fact that she was pregnant! I never knew that about them!" They both laughed. "It was funny to read about some of the people she mentioned. Roderick was with me until about ten years ago. He was very smart. Once I brought on Lee to be the general manger, Roderick focused on managing our finances. Not bad for someone whose father had been a slave."

"Unbelievable! I remember Dede writing about that, but I didn't know he'd grown up to be so successful. And what about Maddie's friend being named Chloe, just like our Chloe? That's a coincidence."

"Yeah. And Alexander, the guy from Greece whom my dad delivered. I'm still friends with him. We'll have to go see him. His kids are grown now, but he and his wife still live in Long Beach."

"What about your mom's son and daughter?" I've never heard you mention them?"

"They've never been interested in me and I've never pursued a relationship with them. John, my brother, died a few years ago. I went to the funeral and talked to my sister and nieces and nephews. They all live in Los Angeles. They're all pretty decent, all except my sister. She's never forgiven my mom for converting to Catholicism and she hated my dad for asking her to do so. She's an old prude. She was even an old prude when she was young. But there is someone I do want you to meet. My step-niece, who I call Aunt Maddie."

"Why do you call your niece Aunt Maddie?"

"Because she's 22 years older than I am. She's Dede's granddaughter. Of course, growing up I didn't know about Dede and I never questioned how Maddie was related to me. We'll go up and see her, soon."

"Where does she live?"

"The Hollywood Hills. She was raised rich and she married rich. You're gonna love her!"

"So, let's see. She's about 70. Just like my mother."

Chapter 20

May 27
The Supreme Court rules 7-1 that burning a draft card is not an act of free speech protected by the First Amendment.

The windows were being replaced in the big bedroom, and the heating and air was being installed, so Alex and Rose decided to retreat to Laguna Beach for several days. On the way home, they visited her parents so Alex could finally meet her father.

"It's just amazing that Dede's journals and my grandmother's memoir have come together and found their place with the two of you!" exclaimed Edna. They were in the parlor of the old Colonial Revival house in Placentia, which Carolina and her husband had built and where Rose had grown up. "It truly is!" she repeated.

"I haven't read your grandmother's memoir, but from what Rose tells me your grandmother was an amazing woman," said Alex.

"Oh she was. You know, she grew up in the days where the only means of travel was by horse, then trains, and she lived to see airplanes crossing the sky."

"I know. My mom and dad were the same. So much happened in their lives."

"I loved reading about the fashions. The men were so manly and the women were so feminine," added Rose.

"They were different times," said Edna. Changing the subject, she said, "Your home project sure is a big undertaking! You'll have to have some big event where people will come down and stay for the weekend," Edna suggested.

"Oh Alex! Wouldn't that be fun? Maybe a Christmas party! Like the ones Dede describes in her journals!"

"I'm not sure the house will be ready by then, honey."

"We'll make certain it is!" At this proclamation, Rose's father came in. "Dad, this is Alex. Alex MacKenzie. Alex, this is my dad, Robert Lefebre." The men shook hands and Robert took a seat close to Alex.

"Beer, Alex?"

"Yeah, that'd be great." Robert went into the kitchen and came back with two bottles of Miller High Life.

"Well Rose, dear, I guess you and I are going to have to take care of ourselves!" Rose and Edna went into the kitchen in search of something other than beer. Rose found a bottle of Merlot and Edna poured herself a glass of water. "Rose, you're glowing."

"I love him, Mom. I really do. I've never felt like this before. And he's so good to me."

"He seems like he would be good for you. He seems, well, calming. I think he could ground you."

"What? You think I need grounding?" But Rose was teasing her mom. "No, Mom, you're right. He's made me reconsider what I've been doing, or more to the point, not doing with my life."

Robert drove Alex around what used to be the property. By now, most of the land had been sold and was being subdivided into housing tracts. "It was the right decision," said Robert. "None of the kids or grandkids wanted to take over the farming, and the land is more valuable for sale than it is for farming nowadays anyway." As the men talked, they drove by one development that was just getting underway. Huge earthmovers were digging, moving, and flattening the earth, readying it for the houses that would be built on top of it. At another site, the houses were already framed and roofers could be seen crawling around on top of them laying shingles.

"I'm sure they'll be nice houses. But look how close together they are. And hardly any yards, front or back," Alex observed.

"Not my cup of tea either," agreed Robert.

With the help of her housekeeper, Edna had made a Peruvian dish, in honor of her grandmother.

The main dish was *carapulcra*, stewed pork and chicken, potatoes, red chilis, and cumin. Accompanying this was a large bowl of *arroz con pollo* and a large platter of *empanadas* filled with a mixture of shredded beef, onions, olives, and chopped boiled eggs. "This was a favorite meal when I was growing up," said Rose.

"Still is," added Robert.

"Rose, do you know how to cook like this?" inquired Alex.

"Well, uh, I, uh..."

"She will!" interjected Edna. Once again, they found themselves enjoying a good laugh.

Chapter 21

June 3
Andy Warhol is shot and critically wounded in his New York City loft by Valerie Solanas, apparently for losing a copy of a play she'd written. She pleads guilty to assault and spends three years in prison.

I just can't believe it!" Rose had been listening to the radio in her studio and was now sharing the news with Alex.

"Did you want to go back there?" Alex didn't really want her to go, but he thought he should offer.

"Oh no. He wouldn't have any idea who I was."

"Sure he would. He wanted you to be in one of his films."

"He was being nice. I only met him one time. I was in New York and a friend and I somehow got invited to the Factory. I was flirting with him and he was being nice, that's all. But I will send a note. I'm sure he'll get cards from all over the world. It sounds like he's going to survive."

"I'm going back to Wyoming in a couple of weeks. Want to go?"

"Would you be too disappointed if I said no? I've gotta stay here and stay on these workers. They can't waste a minute if we're going to have this place ready in time for our Christmas Party."

"You think you'll be ok here in the house, alone?"

"I don't know why not."

"I'll leave you one of my guns. You can keep it with you when you're alone in the house or out on the property."

"I don't want a gun. I don't trust myself."

"Well what then? You need protection. How about a dog?"

"A dog? I don't know if I want a dog."

"My dad always had Newfoundlands. You know what they are?"

"They're huge! And I remember Dede writing about their Newfoundland. I think they called him Newton the Great."

"Yeah. That would have been his first one. The one we had when I was a kid was Bruno. I loved him. Good protection. I'll see what I can do about it."

The road continued up, twisting and turning throughout the hills and offering spectacular views of the Los Angeles basin below. On some turns, they could see Catalina Island basking in the sparkling blue waters just off the coast. They had taken the 101 freeway, locally known as the Hollywood Freeway, and exited at Hollywood Blvd. From there they had driven west to La Brea Avenue, where they turned north and headed up into the Hollywood Hills. They were on their way to visit Alex's Aunt Maddie and her husband.

"Oh my God, look at you!" Maddie was exuberant as she opened the door. But Rose was surely more surprised than Maddie was. Rose had figured her to be 70 years old, but she looked more like 50, if that. Even her hands didn't betray her age, lacking any age spots or wrinkles or any other tell-tale signs of having been used for 70 years. *I guess this is what being married to a world-famous plastic surgeon gets you*, Rose thought to herself.

"And who is this you've brought to meet me? Must be someone pretty special, since you've never

brought anyone else up here to meet me!" Maddie
carried on about how good it was to see Alex and how it
had been too long and other well-meaning, truthful
cliches people say when they haven't seen someone in a
long time.

Maddie walked them into her home, where they
entered into the living room. It was a huge, open-space
step-down room, upholstered, carpeted, and painted all
in white. The large coffee table was glass. On it sat a
plate of chocolate bon bons, a tall gold cigarette lighter,
and a beautiful crystal ash tray. Alex handed her the
basket of oranges and two bottles of wine they had
brought with them. Before they sat down, he and Maddie
strolled over to the window, which took up the entire
south wall of the living room. In the afternoon sun, they
could see the entire Los Angeles basin, with its high-rise
buildings, parks, neighborhoods, and swimming pools.
To the west, they could see the ocean. It was a stunning
view, and Maddie promised that it was even more
stunning when the sun went down and millions of lights
lit up the city.

"So come have a seat and tell me what you've
been up to. Ron will be home any time now." So they
told her about the renovations, the museum, and Alex's
work with the mustangs. They told her about Rose's
involvement with the residents of the half-way house and
a little about her family's history. Maddie was amazed
that Rose's great-grandmother actually knew her own
grandmother, Dede. They talked about Dede's journals
and Carolina's memoir.

"Maddie, what was your grandmother like?" ventured Alex.

"Oh my, how can I describe her? I didn't like her, you know."

"What? I had no idea! Why not?"

"Oh I was very jealous of her. I had a crush on your father since the day I met him. I was only about 5 years old. To me, my grandmother was just someone who was in the way." They all chuckled. "But actually, she was very nice. And beautiful, I'll give her that."

"She seems to have been quite accomplished," added Rose.

"Oh, that she was. She was larger than life, she was. Beautiful, smart, accomplished, talented, kind, you name it, she was it. I always thought of her as something like a goddess. And because she was a goddess, she was not someone you could get very close to."

"Really?" inquired Alex. "My dad didn't seem to have any trouble approaching her."

"Of course not. He was a god!" Again, they chuckled. "They really were an amazing couple, reigning over their kingdom from their temple on the ranch. But they were very good people, very generous, and never looked down their noses at people who didn't have as much. Bigger than life, though. That's what I say. Way bigger than life."

"My mother wasn't like that. She was just an ordinary woman. I loved her of course, but I've never understood why my father married her, especially so soon after Dede died. Although recently I found something she wrote that indicated she was pregnant when they got married."

Maddie laughed. "Well, that she was. As you know, I was close to your mother. I went down there when you were born and helped her out for a couple of months. I got to know her quite well then, and we remained close until the day she died."

"I know my father loved her. I just don't know why he chose someone so different than his first wife."

"Your father didn't marry until he was in his 50s. I think that he discovered he liked being married, and when Dede died he didn't want to be alone for the rest of his life."

"But why my mom?"

"Your mom was a lovely woman, Alex. She wasn't a goddess; she was a mortal. He fell in love with a mortal. And she was a very attractive woman. Where Dede shimmered and sparkled, your mother radiated a warm glow. Don't underestimate her attraction."

Rose noticed Alex's eyes were moist, but he didn't allow a tear to fall. "Thank you, Maddie," was all he said.

Ron came home and introductions were made. "How is your sister doing, Alex? We're sorry we didn't make it to your brother's funeral, but as you know we were traveling in Scandinavia at the time."

Maddie added, "I don't think Laura would have wanted us there anyway, dear. She always considered me trash. Is she still involved with the church, Alex?"

"Oh yes. They live like paupers. Seems to think it's a requirement of being holy. I haven't seen her since John's funeral. She thinks I'm trash too!" They all laughed.

A woman wearing an apron came out and spoke quietly to Maddie, informing her that dinner would be ready in a few minutes. They moved to the dining room, where a staff of three waited on them. "I do hope you like lobster, but I know not everyone does. If that's the case, I hope the filet mignon will be enough." The steak and lobster were preceded by a lovely green salad, then accompanied by asparagus spears and baked potatoes. Each of the diners had their choice of red or white wine. The conversation was easy and uninterrupted throughout the dinner. "What do you say we have our dessert outside?" suggested Maddie. "It's a lovely evening."

They moved out to the backyard and sat at a table next to the swimming pool. The perimeter of the yard was planted in lush, tropical plants. Bougainvillea grew on a fence surrounding the yard. Bird of Paradise, fuchsias, geraniums, lantana, and other beautifully colored flowers were abundant. From this vantage point, they could see some of the city. Maddie had been right. The night lights of Los Angeles were spectacular. They ate their lavender-flavored crème brulee and soaked in the warm ambience of Maddie's house in the Hollywood Hills.

On the drive back to Riverside, Rose and Alex didn't talk much. Both were reflecting on the conversation they had enjoyed with Maddie and Ron.

Chapter 22

June 4
*Robert F. Kennedy, gaining momentum in his
presidential campaign, wins the California primary –
and is assassinated at the Ambassador Hotel in Los
Angeles. Gunman Sirhan Sirhan, a Jordanian citizen of
Palestinian descent, is captured at the scene.*

The country is going to hell," exclaimed Alex. All the
major news stations were carrying the story from the
time their transmitters were turned on at 6:00 A.M.
until they quit broadcasting at midnight. Once again,
the country was in mourning, and shock.

"I just can't believe it," answered Rose. "First
President Kennedy and now him. And right here in our
own back yard!"

"I'm going to postpone my trip to Wyoming for
a couple of weeks, wait 'til the country gets back to
some kind of normal."

"Good. I'd rather you never gather up any more wild horses. I saw that movie."

"What? What movie?"

"The one with Clark Gable and Marilyn Monroe. It was horrible what they did to those horses. I think they were mustangs."

"You're talking about *The Misfits*? They were inhumane. They captured them for slaughter to use for dog food. That's not what I do."

"But still. It's the same thing."

"No it's not. The herds are way over-populated. Wild horses die a slow death, succumbing to starvation. What I'm doing is helping. We bring them back, break them, then sell them to people who'll cherish them and give them a good home. As a matter of fact, the Bureau of Land Management is drafting a plan to regulate the humane capture of these animals, specifically to save the herd and allow them to graze on land that is plentiful for smaller herds. I don't want to hear any more about it."

A few days later, Alex came home with a Newfoundland and presented him to Rose. He was seven weeks old, and they named him Fitzgerald. Chloe and Heidi fell madly in love with him, giving him table scraps and feeding him foods that the breeder had explicitly told Alex not to feed him. Fitz lapped up all the food and love he could get. He was smart, too. He was house trained after just one accident, and he learned his way around the house within the first couple of hours. Rose absolutely loved him, even allowing him up on the bed with her; that is, until Alex discovered him up there and resolutely put his foot down. From then on Fitz slept on the floor on Rose's side of the bed. He often jumped up onto the seat of Alex's truck as he made his way around the property. In no time at all, he was a regular member of the family.

They focused on the house. All of the furniture had arrived the week before. Rose loved the rich look of the gold sectional and matching gold, silk rug. The striped satin drapes and matching chairs brought more of the color palate into the room, and the conversation area by the front window had turned out exactly the way she wanted it to look.

In front of the sectional was a large kidney-shape table with tapered legs that matched the legs on the satin chairs. On this, Rose placed the cluster of grapes she had made. In her studio, she had molded 2- and 3-inch round ornaments out of resin and attached them to a twig of wood. She had chosen shades of orange for the resin to complement the room's décor. She and Alex had also purchased a stereo and television console that matched the wood of the coffee table. The console had doors that slid closed to hide the tv, radio, and turntable equipment, and the flat surface provided another area on which to display photographs and curios. This console was placed to the right of the fireplace, under the window.

Rose loved the natural element of George Nakashima's tables. However, Mac had made the large dining room table himself, and it rather resembled a Nakashima, with its thick tabletop and unfinished sides, which by now were worn smooth with time. She purchased 12 of Nakashima's straight-back chairs to set around the table. On one of the dining room walls she displayed a collection of six Ansel Adams' black and white photographs, all of Yosemite.

Rose proclaimed the kitchen and living room, including the dining room, to be absolutely perfect. Alex agreed and gave her a loving kiss. "I knew I hired the right person when I found you," he said.

The two rooms off the living room, Alex's office and the other unused room, got an update too. Alex's office was painted a pale green and the bookshelves were sanded and painted in white enamel. The large desk and file cabinets were left in their original dark wood, which leant an air of masculinity to the room. Mac's medical school degree and his degree from West Point, along with Alex's MBA from Princeton, hung on the wall behind the desk. A large Aubusson carpet, similar to the one in the conversation area of the living room, was lain on the floor and tied the office to the rest of the downstairs space. Rose surprised him by bringing home a small, portable television and setting it up on the top of one of the file cabinets, adjusting the rabbit ears to bring in reception. She encouraged him to watch tv in here instead of in the living room, which she declared was off-limits for daily television viewing and beer drinking.

Alex told her the other room should be hers. She wasn't sure what to use it for, as she already had the two-room guest house to use as a studio. One of the rooms had the kiln in it, but the other room could certainly be used as an office, if she ever had need for one. She had it painted the same pale green to match Alex's office and brought in another Aubusson in complementary colors. She just wasn't sure what she'd do with the room.

Soon after the room was painted, Rose was talking to her mother on the phone and telling her about the space. Her mother suggested she turn it into her own personal library and reading area. Edna surprised her when she offered, "And if you'd like it, you can have my grandmother's escritoire. It would look beautiful in a room like that!"

"Mother, are you kidding me? You'd give that to me?"

"Of course. That is, if you think you're going to be staying there."

"I hope so, Mom. I mean, we're not talking marriage yet, but don't you think the fact that he's given me a guest house and an office inside that he must be thinking this is permanent?"

"I'd think so, honey, but I can't keep up with all the new rules of your generation. I'm still trying to get used to the idea that my little girl is living with a man whom she's not married to."

"I'm sorry Mom. I know that must bother you."

"Well, I'm glad you're happy. I have something else for you when you come to get the desk. My grandmother's husband bought her a gorgeous hand-blown glass bowl. You know the one, it's always been in our dining room."

"Yes, it's beautiful! You'd give that to me? I don't know what to say!"

"All of this stuff is going to be yours someday anyway. You might as well have it now. The blown glass bowl would look so nice on that console you've told me about it. But you can put it anywhere you want."

"The colors are perfect. It's got swirls of oranges and reds, doesn't it?"

"That's it. Jerry told her it represented her orange groves. It's yours now, honey."

Chapter 23

June 19
*The efforts of the Poor People's Campaign climaxes in
the Solidarity Day Rally for Jobs, Peace, and Freedom
in Washington, D.C. Fifty thousand people join the
3,000 participants living at Resurrection City on the
National Mall to rally around the demands of the Poor
People's Campaign on Solidarity Day.*

I think Lord Henry represents the devil," suggested
Larry.

"I agree," chimed in Paul. "He tempted Dorian
with his own hedonistic evil."

"But Dorian made his own decisions. Just
because someone offers you temptations, doesn't mean
you have to act on them. We all have a free will."

Pamela refused to blame Dorian's bad decisions on Lord Henry.

The Picture of Dorian Gray had turned out to be a hit with the residents, not so much for its artistic value but for its literary value. She had presented it to them as a book about ideas, a book that asked questions about beauty and the relationships among art, life, and consequences. She meant for them to concentrate on what the book had to say about art. But the group went way beyond that.

She had not expected them to be so moved by the book. Truthfully, she had not expected them to be so academic about it. She admitted to herself, and later to Alex, that their interpretations of the novel were much more profound than her own.

After the group talk, Pamela asked Rose if she'd like to come up to her room for a cup of tea, and Rose accepted. Entering the room, she was taken by how nice it was. The room had a south-facing window that allowed for a lot of light. Pamela's plant, hanging in its macraméd hanger, was flourishing. It was at least twice the size it was when she planted it. The bed, occasional chair, and small dinette set were shabby, but she had draped some pretty floral fabric over them and had made a big improvement. A large doily was placed on the chair as a headrest. An empty milk bottle held freshly cut flowers. Pamela told her she had planted a flower garden in the yard in back of the home. A picture of Jesus hung on the wall. On a table next to the chair was a photograph of two young boys, about 8 and 10 years old. "This is lovely, Pamela. Are these your sons?"

"Yes. They're much older now though. But that's the only picture of them I have."

"I see. Do you see them often?"

"Oh no. No, my husband makes sure of that."

"What happened, Pamela. If you don't want to tell me, I understand."

"Oh gosh, where do I begin?" Pamela told a story of a young woman who was raised in a lower-income family. At 19, she met a charming young man, a man from a wealthy family and who was finishing law school. Against the wishes of his family, but to the incredibly proud joy of her own family, they married shortly after they met.   "Looking back, I guess he was trying to rebel against his family. But in the end, he turned out to be just like them." They had two children and he found his niche as a divorce lawyer. The money flowed, and Pamela was blissfully happy. She never would have thought that she would have a beautiful house, a handsome husband who loved her, and two adorable sons. After about 15 years, when he became romantically involved with a woman in his office, another divorce lawyer, and wanted his own divorce, Pamela hadn't stood a chance. With a facility borne out of years of helping men get out of their marriages without losing more than 5% of their assets, he got the house, his entire income, the kids, the cars, their vacation home, their investment savings, and a new wife. She got $4000 to start a new life.

The money was gone before her new life started. The furnished apartment was $560 per month, and she'd had to buy some bed linens and toiletries. "I was really dumb. I had moved from my parents' house into my husband's family's home, then into our own home, and had never really learned to manage money. My husband took care of all our finances." Consequently, the money was gone within a few months and she was evicted from the apartment. Pleas to her family went unheeded. They were ashamed of her. They had bragged to everyone they knew that their daughter had married an attorney from a wealthy family, and now she had brought them shame. During this time, she made repeated pleas to her husband to let her see her sons, but when he threatened to get a restraining order against her, she gave up.

She found herself on the street. The first night she went to the Rescue Mission in downtown Los Angeles. When she awoke in the morning her purse was gone. She moved from there to a shelter for women, but was harassed because she didn't fit in. She started sleeping in the doorway of the public library. It was on the steps of the library where she noticed a woman whose purse was hanging open, and in it was the checkbook, just there for the taking. So she took it.

The first time she attempted to cash a check she was arrested. The public defender convinced her to take a plea deal, which would reduce the time she would serve from twelve years down to two or three. She served two years and 10 months, and now she was out, a convicted felon with no prospects of getting a job. Her husband was granted the restraining order right after she'd been arrested.

"How long do you think you'll be here?" asked Rose, politely.

"A while longer. I'm working with Pastor Hartgrove on forgiveness. Of my husband and myself."

"Pamela, I'm so sorry for the turn of events you've suffered in your life. It seems like your husband should be made to pay!"

"Hah! That's not what forgiveness is about, my dear Rose. I'm working on that."

As Rose drove home that afternoon she tried to think of a way she might help Pamela. But nothing came to mind.

On the way home she stopped at a music store to buy some 45s for the new console. It would hold up to twelve singles at a time, automatically releasing the next record as soon as the previous record was over. She had noticed that Alex's collection was scant and mostly consisted of big band 78s and some country western music. She looked through the stacks of records and chose some current songs: *I'm a Believer* by The Monkees; *To Sir with Love* by Lulu; Aretha Franklin's *Respect; Ruby Tuesday* by the Rolling Stones; Van Morrison's *Brown Eyed Girl;* The Beatles' *Hey Jude;* Otis Reddings' *Sittin' on the Dock of the Bay; I Wish it*

Would Rain by The Temptations; *Grazing in the Grass* by Hugh Masekela; *It's a Beautiful Morning* by The Young Rascals; *Ain't Nothing Like the Real Thing* by Marvin Gaye and Tammi Terrell; and *Do You Know the Way to San Jose* by Dionne Warwick. There were others she would like to have had, songs by The Doors and The Jefferson Airplane, but she thought she'd be pressing her luck with Alex.

Alex was in Wyoming rounding up another dozen or two wild mustangs. Edna had come to stay with Rose and had brought the escritoire and glass-blown bowl with her. "Honey, this house is beautiful!" They carried the desk into Rose's library and set it in the middle of the room. Edna had brought the chair that went with it too but wasn't sure Rose would actually want it. They both decided it was perfect, but the cushion needed new fabric. The room now had a loveseat under the window. It was upholstered in a fabric that was reminiscent of Monet's garden. Robby had arranged to build floor-to-ceiling bookshelves on one of the walls. These were painted white to match those in Alex's office in the adjoining room. The effect was light, feminine, and inviting. "You're going to have to start filling these shelves," her mother told her.

They went into Riverside in search of a remnant of fabric to cover the old chair cushion. They found a piece of dark green damask that they both agreed would be perfect. Once home, Rose sat on the loveseat while her mother removed the old fabric and wrapped the new around the cushion, stapling and tacking it into place. "I believe my grandmother would approve," exclaimed Edna when the job was done.

On Saturday night Edna asked about the local Catholic church, and Rose had to admit to her that she didn't know anything about it because she hadn't been there. A quick look in the phone book told them the church in Rubidoux was called St. John the Evangelist. The next morning she accompanied her mother to Mass. It was a nice church, only a few years old, light and airy, with a modern altar. In keeping with Vatican II, the priest faced the congregants, and the Mass was said in English, rather than in Latin. Rose immediately felt at home and intended to return, possibly every Sunday. They went out to lunch after Mass, and shortly after they returned to the ranch Edna left for home.

Late that night Alex arrived home with his entourage, including six horse trailers carrying four horses each. Rose quickly got redressed and went outside to watch the commotion. She hopped up into Alex's truck and rode with him to the corral. She stood back and watched the practiced and strategic unloading of the wild horses. Some of them bucked and reared up on their hind legs, unfamiliar with the environment and unwilling to be led into a space with a fence encircling it. She felt sorry for them but remembered what Alex had told her about this being in their best interest.

When his trailer had been unloaded, he drove her back to the house, then returned to help unload the rest of the horses. He arrived back at the house about 1:00 A.M., took a shower, and crawled in bed, taking Rose in his arms. "I missed you, beautiful woman." Within seconds Rose realized how much she had missed him, too. They made up for the time apart, then fell asleep in each other's arms.

Chapter 24

July 1
Johnson signs the Treaty on the Non-Proliferation of Nuclear Weapons, which remains the world's primary means of preventing the spread of nuclear weapons to non-nuclear states and reducing nuclear weapons in the world.

Alex and Rose had decided to forego redoing the master bedroom to assure that all the guest rooms would be done in time for the Christmas party. But Robby told them that he could hire two or three subcontractors, each with their own full crews, to do the work simultaneously. One crew was assigned the master bedroom and four of the guest rooms, and the other two crews were assigned seven guest rooms each. Work had begun three weeks before and by now was well underway. The nineteen guest rooms would be done in three different color schemes, each scheme being repeated in six nonconsecutive rooms. One color scheme included turquoise, golds, and lime green. Another scheme included orange, red, and pale turquoise. The third color scheme was pink, lavender, and pale turquoise. Every guest room already had a dresser and/or an armoire. In each room, one of these pieces of heavy wooden furniture would be stripped down and repainted in one of the colors of the scheme, then finished with an antiquing technique. Alex wasn't happy about the old furniture being repainted, but he acquiesced to Rose, knowing that she knew best. Anyway, he figured they could always be re-stripped and re-stained in their original natural wood stain.

That's amazing, Jay!" They had used a black permanent marker to draw a lion's face, and now they were coloring them in with wide-tipped permanent color markers. Most of the residents had reached for the browns, yellows, and golds. Jay had reached for golds, greens, and purples. The result was stunning. "May I take a picture of it?"

From their first lesson, Rose had taken pictures of the students' products. She framed them and hung them in her studio at home. Every time she added a new one she chuckled to herself, as they reminded her of Mac hanging up his sketches of Dede. But Rose's photos weren't racy; they simply made a very nice photo array of the art she had been teaching at the halfway house.

Pamela stayed to help Rose clean up the multipurpose room. "Would you like to come up for a cup of tea before you get on the road, Rose?"

As they entered Pamela's room, Rose was once again taken aback by how much the plant had grown. "I swear, Pamela, your fern is twice the size it was the last time I was here! You must have one heck of a green thumb!"

Pamela laughed, and when she did the years melted away, transforming her face into the pretty girl she must once have been. "I've always been pretty good with plants. I used to dream of having my own flower business."

"Really? You mean a florist shop?"

"Not so much that. I wanted to be the person who grew the flowers, then, you know, sold them to the florists."

"Maybe you still can."

"No, I'm afraid that time has come and gone. Actually, I worry about what I'm going to do when I move out of here. Pastor Hargrove is looking into a few options."

Rose was sitting in the living room with a glass of chilled, white wine, enjoying the beautiful décor and congratulating herself on her work. She never ceased to be amazed at the original Monet that hung above the fireplace. She sure would like to have known Mac and Dede. They must have been one captivating couple, she mused.

She had added to her growing collection of 45s and albums. She had put on a stack of twelve singles, the maximum for this phonograph. It always amazed her how the changer could move the arm out of the way for the record to drop, them move the arm back in to set the stylus on the record. The Young Rascals' *Groovin' on a Sunday Afternoon* had just dropped down when Alex walked down the stairs and into the living room. He extended his arm to her in an invitation to dance. Rose's heart fluttered as she stood up and moved into his arms. He was a wonderful dancer, and the temperate beat of the song made it easy for her to follow him. When the song ended, he held her in his arms for several more minutes before walking her back to the sofa. "I'm going to get a beer. Can I get you some more wine?" he asked.

"No, I'm good," she answered, her heart just now settling back to its normal rhythm. The next record to magically drop down was Herb Alpert's *This Guy's in Love with You*. The serendipity of it made her smile. She thought now might be a good time to tell Alex about Pamela and ask him about her plans.

"Rose, honey, we can't take in stray people. We have no idea what this woman is like, what she's done, what she might do. No, we can't do that." Alex was adamant.

"Yes, we do. Anway, I do. She found herself in a hopeless situation and made a bad decision. She's not a bad person, Alex. She's very nice. And you can't imagine what she does with plants!"

"What do I care about what she does with plants?"

"She could grow flowers for us, Alex. She could transform the yard into a showcase of flowers and provide the flowers we'll need for the house. Remember, we'll need to have a standing order to keep the vases full of fresh flowers every week. She could do that for us."

"What exactly do you have in mind? You want her to live here with us? That doesn't sit well with me."

"She could live in my studio. I haven't done anything with the second bedroom yet. We could give her a small plot of land and see what she does. If she's as good as I think she is, maybe you could work out some sort of a business deal with her. And when she's not tending to the flowers, she could help Heidi and Chloe."

"Are we expected to pay her? I mean, we're giving her a free room. Are we expected to feed her too?"

"I don't know, Alex!" Rose raised her voice in frustration. She hadn't expected Alex to be so reticent to her idea, which she thought benefited everyone.

"Let me meet her."

Chapter 25

July 18

Gordon Moore and Robert Noyce incorporate their microprocessor manufacturing firm. After rejecting the name "Moore Noyce" as too close to "more noise," they eventually settle on Intel.

The work in the guest rooms was speeding along much more quickly than Alex and Rose anticipated, speed that Alex credited to Robby. Robby didn't have a wife or children, and it seemed he devoted his life to his work. He was there by 6:00 every morning and stayed until about 6:00 every evening. Most mornings he and Alex sat down at the kitchen table and went over the plans for the day. It seemed to Rose that Robby had become a part of the family. Alex was pleased that the job site was always tidy. Sawdust swept up, electrical cables coiled, everything cleaned up before the workers went home every day.

They had decided on a turquoise, green, and rose color scheme for the master bedroom. Rose thought the turquoise and green would be masculine enough for Alex, and the rose would add a touch of femininity for her, or at least for some woman, maybe in the future. She really didn't know where she fit in to this house. Alex had never mentioned marriage. If he did, would she want to marry him? He was very much into doing his own thing, as the current phrase went. He seemed to be happy that she was there, but somehow she got the feeling that he would be just as happy if she wasn't. Should she talk to him about it?

As work got underway in the master bedroom, Alex and Rose moved to her house in Laguna Beach. They planned to stay for two, maybe three, weeks. It was July, hot, and it was a nice reprieve to be out of Riverside and on the coast, where there was always a cool ocean breeze. They took daily walks on the beach and Alex took morning swims in the ocean. Rose cooked healthy, natural food for dinner most nights, and when they didn't eat at home they ate at any of the beachside cafes and restaurants that Laguna had to offer. At home they read, watched tv, went in the spa, and made love any time the mood hit them, morning, noon, or night.

"Why don't you give up the lease on your studio space?" inquired Alex.

"I don't know. I might need it."

"Why would you need it? You have a great studio at home."

"That's your home, Alex. Not mine."

Several minutes of silence passed. "I want it to be your home too, Rose. I mean, you've completely redecorated it the way you want it. If I didn't plan on you being there, I sure wouldn't have chosen those colors!"

Rose looked at him with a look of dismay, threw her wine glass across the room, shattering it against the wall, ran into the bedroom, slammed the door, and burst into tears. Alex was dumbfounded. He left her alone to her sobs until he sensed they were subsiding, then walked into the bedroom and sat on the bed. "Was it something I said?" he asked, tentatively.

"Get out of here!"

"Uh, ok, I guess I didn't go about that very tactfully, did I?"

"Why don't you just go back to your house, your ranch, your horses, your everything! None of it has anything to do with me! I guess I'm just your temporary, what, your temporary mistress? Your temporary girlfriend? You'll dump me as soon as someone else comes along, just like you dumped Donna when you met me!" She started crying again, deep sobs with her face buried in the pillow.

Alex allowed ten minutes of silence to go by. Finally, he swung his feet up onto the bed and sat up against the headboard. "Rose, would you sit up and talk to me?"

"I want you to leave."

"Well I'm not leaving. I want to talk to you."

"Then talk."

"I want you to sit up so I can see you." Finally, Rose sat up, still trying to take a deep breath, her eyes red and swollen.

Alex put his finger under her chin and lifted her face so he could see her. "I love you. *Mi casa es su casa.* Isn't that what your grandmother would have said?" Alex laughed at himself.

"My great-grandmother, and you're not funny."

"No, I guess I'm not. I want you in my house forever. And it will no longer be my house. It's our house."

"Alex, I know it's 1968 and there's a sexual revolution going on, but I don't want to be a part of it. I'm already living with a man, having sex with him, who I'm not married to. Do you think that's what I want? Well it's not!"

Several minutes of silence elapsed. "I've been putting this off because we're so different. You're a left-wing hippy; I'm a conservative war vet. You're an artist; I'm a rancher. You're young; I'm old. You're Laguna Beach; I'm Riverside. But even with all those differences, Rose, I love you. I want to spend the rest of my life with you." Once again, he used his finger to lift her face so he could look into her eyes. "Rose, will you marry me?"

Rose stared at him. Her stomach flip-flopped. "It's what I want more than anything, Alex. Yes, I'll marry you."

They found a jeweler in Newport Beach to make custom rings for them. Rose chose a 2.5 carat solitaire marquis diamond in a platinum setting for her engagement ring. The wedding band had a series of .25 carat diamonds embedded in platinum. Alex's wedding band was platinum with a .5 carat marquis embedded in it. "But you know I can't wear this every day while I'm working with the horses or out in the orchard," he admitted.

"Oh, I know, silly. But you will wear it when we go out, right?"

"Proudly."

"And for your information, I'm not a left-wing hippy." Alex raised his eyebrows, then they both laughed. "Aren't you supposed to ask my father for permission, or something?"

"You're 32 years old, Rose. Do you think you really need your father's permission?"

"Well, I mean, he's kind of old-fashioned."

"If you must know, I already asked him."

"What?" she asked, astonished to hear this.

"That day we went out to drive around what used to be your property. I told him I loved you, and asked him if he'd be ok if someday I asked you to marry me?"

"You did? What did he say?"

"He got out his checkbook and offered me $10,000 to take you off his hands."

Rose looked bewildered. Then she realized he was kidding. "Oh he did not!"

"No, imp. But he did give me his blessing. Now you can call and tell them it's official." He put his arm around her as they walked to the car.

They drove back to Riverside so Rose could teach her class. Alex accompanied her so he could meet Pamela. While Pamela was wiping down the tables after class, Alex pulled Rose off to the side and inquired, "Are you sure you want to do this?"

He went into the office and met with Pastor Hartgrove. The pastor told him he had several feelers out for a place for Pamela to live and several others for a place where she could work. Alex told him of his and Rose's plan. Because of the contract Shepherd Ministries had with the county, Pastor Hartgrove would need to see the accommodations and approve of both the living conditions and the work arrangements. They agreed that he would come out to the ranch the following week.

They stopped off at the ranch, picked up a few more pieces of clothing and essentials, checked the progress of the work, and headed back to Laguna Beach.

On the drive home, Rose proclaimed, "I'd like to start going to church."

"Then you should."

"No, I mean with you."

"I'm afraid the walls would fall down if I went to church. I haven't set foot in one in over twenty years."

"Well, I can't claim to be very devout myself, but I want to be. My mother, her grandmother, they both found such comfort in it. Dede did too. And your own mother was a convert. In reading Dede's journals, it sounded like your father was involved with the Catholic church too. I'd really like to give it a try."

That Sunday they went to Mass at the mission in San Juan Capistrano, in honor of Rose's great grandmother and only a few miles from Laguna Beach. Contrary to Alex's prediction, the walls of the church did not fall down. As a matter of fact, he enjoyed the service. They both did and agreed to give their local church in Rubidoux a try.

Chapter 26

July 23

In Cleveland, the Glenville Shootout, between police and black militants, leaves three dead on each side, plus one bystander. Riots rock the city for five days. Mayor Carl Stokes, seven months into his term as the first black official to lead a major U.S. city, later writes, "That night was to haunt and color every aspect of my administration."

They returned to the ranch to meet Pastor Hartgrove. They showed him the guest house that Rose used as her studio that had an available bedroom for Pamela. Pastor Hartgrove had a check-off list and was able to check off all the requirements: bathroom, kitchen, sleeping quarters, clean, healthy environment, etc. Both the pastor and Alex signed on the dotted line and agreed that Pamela would join them the following week.

Back in Laguna Beach, Rose relinquished the lease on her studio space. While she was there, an acquaintance informed her that Kyle had been arrested again. She was astonished to hear that once again the charges were for the same thing for which he had previously been arrested. "The pigs must have been surveilling his house, man, just waiting for him to do something wrong," the woman told her. This time he wasn't given bail; he would wait out the trial from a jail cell.

Rose hadn't told her parents yet about the engagement. She wanted to tell them in person. So the day after they picked up their rings, she called her parents and asked them to come to dinner. As soon as Edna and Robert stepped into the living room, Rose waved her hand in front of them and her mother squealed with delight. "Oh darling, let me see that thing!" Robert gave his daughter a hug and shook Alex's hand. Drinks were poured, hugs went around again, and the excitement was palpable.

"We'll have to have an engagement party!" declared Edna. Rose looked at Alex, who said, "I don't think our place will be finished for some time yet."

"Why don't we keep it small? Just the family," suggested Edna. "We can invite your brothers and their families. Maybe we can just have a dinner at our house."

"I like that," concurred Alex. "How about you, honey?"

"I love the idea. Let's call them right now!" So plans were made for the weekend after next. The brothers would come to Placentia, meet Alex, and celebrate the engagement. Rose felt like she was walking on air. As much as she liked to think of herself as a free spirit, becoming Mrs. Alexander MacKenzie was much more in line with her core values. And, she was in love.

That weekend they went to the Laguna Festival of the Arts, and in the evening they attended the Pageant of the Masters. The pageant had been an annual event since 1933, the year after the Festival began. It showcased masterpieces through large displays on stage featuring live models as the subjects. The performances along with the orchestra, original score, live narration, and intricate sets, provided for a spectacular evening. This year, Rose and Alex were treated to 26 living displays of masterpieces, including Gaugin's *Little Girls of Brittany*; Michelangelo's *La Pieta*; Dega's *Dancers Adjusting their Slippers*; Andrew Wyeth's *Young America*; Norman Rockwell's *Ladies at the Gallery*; Winslow Homer's *Undertow*; and the breathtaking finale, DaVinci's *The Last Supper*. Alex, who had never attended the pageant before, remarked, "That's pretty amazing, isn't it?"

"Every time I come here I'm blown away. You know, all of the people in the living displays are volunteers."

"Is that right? Good for them!"

"That's right. There are about 300 of them."

The following day they attended the Sawdust Festival. Three years earlier, a group of hippy artists had decided to begin their own festival, without any of the long-established juries that critiqued the art featured at the Festival. The Sawdust featured mostly folk art and was decidedly not as sophisticated as the Festival of the Arts taking place across the street. While they were there, a streaker ran naked through the crowd. Hare Krishna members chanted East Indian music and asked for monetary donations. After wandering through the booths for an hour, Alex was ready to leave. Making their way toward the exit, Rose purchased an incense holder and a package of incense, which Alex declared would never be allowed to be burned in their house. Rose laughed at him.

Chapter 27

August 20
The Soviet Union invades Czechoslovakia, halting the Prague Spring.

August 21
Pvt. First Class James Anderson Jr. who died covering an enemy grenade to protect fellow Marines during a firefight in Vietnam, becomes the first African-American Marine to receive the Medal of Honor.

I have to admit, honey, it's beautiful." They had just walked into the master bedroom, completely redone according to Rose's plan.

The walls had been painted a light blue-green. The bedspread was a floral pattern of blues, greens, and pinks. Decorative shams and pillows were a variety of turquoise, blue, green, and rose in both plain and complementary print fabrics. The new, small, sectional in front of the fireplace was turquoise with a diamond-tuck backing, and the chair that was positioned next to it was done in a turquoise and green plaid. The curtains that framed the large sliding glass door, which had been installed to replace the original single door and that led out to the wrap-around balcony, were made from the same fabric as the bedspread. The long dresser next to the bed and the armoire had both been repainted in a light turquoise with an antique finish. A huge wool Aubusson rug was placed under the bed and extended half the length of the bedroom.

The bathroom had been painted the same light turquoise as the bedroom. Towels and rugs in the same turquoise-green-rose color scheme finished the decor. There was even a telephone next to the toilet and another one within reach of the bathtub.

"Yes, indeed, Rose. You've outdone yourself." He pulled her close to him and to show his appreciation gave her a succulent kiss. "I love you, my little imp."

Edna had planned the engagement dinner to be served in the remaining orchard behind the house. The long rustic table had been covered in an elegant tablecloth, beautifully embroidered by her grandmother, Carolina. Her best china and silverware, also inherited from her grandmother, had been set out, along with two beautiful silver candelabras. In addition to the candles, Chinese lanterns had been strategically placed hanging from the trees surrounding the table.

"My grandmother always said this was her favorite setting, a combination of rustic and elegance," she explained.

The meal was Peruvian, also in honor of her grandmother. Edna had hired caterers to serve the meal. It began with an appetizer of *anticucho*, meat marinated in *aji panca*, hot red pepper sauce, skewered on a stick and then grilled. Next, they served a cool quinoa salad. Lightly fried chunks of eggplant, tomatoes, zucchinis, mushrooms, and jalapenos were mixed into the quinoa, then tossed with a mixture of olive oil and an *aji* vinaigrette. Cilantro and arugula were added into this.

La causa was served as a side dish. This was a potato dough layered with shredded chicken, cheese curd, and avocado. The dough was made from mashed potato, ahi pepper and lemon juice. Edna proudly bragged to the dinner table that the potato is originally from Peru, and that all Peruvian dinners feature the vegetable in some form or another.

As soon as the *la causa* was served, the main dish, which had been individually plated, arrived. *Aji de gallina,* a chicken and dish mixed with carrots, celery, leek, breadcrumbs, and milk, and seasoned with olive oil, onion, garlic, *aji*, cumin and turmeric, was served over potato slices and topped with parmesan cheese. Added to each plate were olives, quartered hard boiled eggs, and a baguette.

Edna had cautioned everyone to eat slowly and only take a few bites of the appetizer and side dishes, as the main dish would be quite hardy. But they didn't. Everyone enjoyed every bite of every dish served. By the time the *suspiro limeño* was served everyone was stuffed to the gills. *Suspiro limeño* was a dessert made with caramel, egg yolks, and a meringue made from port wine. It was served in small pudding cups and topped with whipped cream and cinnamon. Even though everyone was way too full, they all ate it.

Rose's brother, John, stood up and gave a toast. They all welcomed Alex into the family and said they felt like they had known him forever. The only problem, John added, was that he should have met his sister ten years ago. This was met with unanimous agreement and a round of laughter. Along with her laughter, Edna shed bittersweet tears. Her baby was getting married.

As Alex was mingling with Edna's extended family, Charlie asked Rose to step aside with him. "I wish you would have called me when you were in trouble."

Rose looked at him in shock. "I don't know what you mean."

"One of the girls who was at your party that night came through our firm. I've read the whole case. You should have come to me, Rose."

Tears flooded her eyes. "I couldn't, Charlie. I was too ashamed. I don't even want to talk about it."

"Look at me, Rose. It isn't even that big of a deal. A lot of people get busted for marijuana. I suspect that one of these days it'll be decriminalized. I just wish you'd have come to me. That's all."

"I'm sorry. Alex helped me."

"I know. I know Novak. He's a good attorney and it looks like he got the charges dropped. That's the important thing."

"Charlie, do you know anything about Kyle? He's my friend whose house we were at."

"From what I understand, he's going down. Maybe could've got a reduced sentence on the first incident, but the idiot went and did it again. I'd say he's looking at at least 5 to 10 years." Rose didn't know what to say or how to react. She couldn't believe that someone so close to her was actually going to prison. She thought of Pamela. "Hey, you ok?"

"Yes. You won't tell Mom and Dad, will you?"

"Of course not. But the next time you need a good attorney, call me." He gave her a hug and they returned to the family.

Alex and Rose celebrated her 33rd birthday quietly. Chloe had made a lovely cake, which they enjoyed after dinner. Alex had set her birthday gifts on the coffee table in the living room, and after the girls had cleaned up the kitchen and left for the evening, he prodded Rose to open them. She could tell that the first gift she reached for was a record album and was delighted to discover it was Simon and Garfunkel's *Book Ends*. "Thank you, Alex. I'm surprised you even knew about this."

"Heidi and Chloe counseled me." The next gift was a hand-blown glass candle holder. It was suspended on a gold chain. "I thought it would look pretty in your office, hanging over your escritoire." When Rose turned to thank him, her eyes reflected a soft glow of love and admiration, admiration that he was so aware of what would please her, and that he had taken the time to purchase this beautiful work of art. The last gift was the biggest, and it was too heavy for her to lift off the table, so she stood and untied the bow and peeled off the paper. The large box held a set of 36 books of classic literature. "To start filling up those empty bookshelves of yours," explained Alex.

"Alex, I don't know what to say. I never would have guessed that you would know to get me the perfect gifts. I'm really just so, so touched. Thank you." She leaned into him for a kiss that became more than a kiss, and necessitated their relocation to the bedroom.

Chapter 28

August 28
At the Democratic National Convention in Chicago, police and Illinois National Guardsmen go on a rampage, clubbing and tear-gassing hundreds of antiwar demonstrators, news reporters and bystanders, with much of the violence broadcast on national TV. The next day, Vice President Hubert Humphrey, perceived as the heir of Johnson's war policies, wins the Democratic nomination, mostly through delegates controlled by party bosses.

The house was finished. Robby suggested it should be featured in *Sunset Magazine* or *Architectural Digest*, but Alex said he didn't want his personal sanctuary splattered across the pages of a magazine and ogled at by readers across the country. Rose was fine with his decision.

Lee was standing outside when Rose pulled into the drive with Pamela in the passenger's seat. "Here, let me get that," he said as Pamela attempted to retrieve her one suitcase and the hanging plant, which by now needed to be repotted. Rose had promised she'd show her how to throw a larger pot on the pottery wheel and to use the kiln.

"Oh, thank you," Pamela responded.

"Lee, this is Pamela. She's going to be staying in the studio. Pamela, this is Lee. He's the general manager who oversees all of Alex's enterprises. Actually, I think we can leave these things in the car. We're just going to go inside for a bit, then I'll drive the car around to the studio and we can unload."

"Nice to meet you, ma'am. You let me know when you're ready and I'll be there to help you unload."

Pamela was speechless when she walked through the front door of the big house. "That's the same reaction I had the first time I saw it," Rose told her, laughing. "Amazing, isn't it?"

"I've never seen anything like it! It's beautiful! And huge! And you say you've recently redecorated it?"

"'Redecorating' is probably an understatement. Alex had all the plumbing and electricity redone. He also put in all new windows and centralized heating and air conditioning. And watch this." She went to the nearest intercom and pressed a button. "Alex, we're home." Alex's voice came out of the box, "OK, be down in a minute."

"That's unbelievable!"

"It is, isn't it?

Heidi and Chloe appeared from the kitchen, anxious to meet the new member of the staff, and Rose introduced them to each other. Pamela was older than the two girls by about fifteen years, but Rose thought they would get along fine.

Alex came down the stairs. For the hundredth time since she'd met him, Rose wondered how any man could be so handsome. He stuck his hand out and shook with Pamela. "Once you get settled, I'd like you to come back in so we can meet in my office."

"Oh, ok," answered Pamela, somewhat unsure of herself. Rose gave Alex a questioning look, which he ignored.

At that same time, Fitz came bounding in, all legs and feet that he still hadn't grown into. He ran circles around Pamela, only stopping when she reached out to scratch him behind his ears. "He's big!" she exclaimed.

"He's a Newfoundland. He's gonna get bigger!" Rose informed her.

Heidi told them that lunch was ready whenever they were, so they sat down at the dining room table and enjoyed grilled cheese sandwiches on sourdough bread, tomato soup, and a fresh green salad.

Afterward, Rose drove Pamela around to the studio, where Lee appeared out of nowhere to help unload her two items. She showed Pamela to the bedroom, which Rose had fixed up with a new full-size bed, bedspread and curtains. "Once you get settled in, you can redecorate to your own liking," she told Pamela.

"Rose, it's beautiful the way it is."

"Well, I'll just leave you two be," muttered Lee as he left.

"He seems nice," Pamela said.

"Oh, he's real nice. He and Alex have been friends since high school. Look, I'll leave you alone here to unpack and look around. I stocked the little fridge with some fruits and cheeses. I wasn't sure if you drink wine, so I didn't include any, but just let me know and I'll bring a bottle of whatever you like."

"I haven't had a glass of wine in several years. I would love a glass of chilled white. But, Rose, I'll just have a glass at some point. I don't need a whole bottle!"

"Ok, I'll leave you alone now. Whenever you're ready, come back up to the house. It's just up the lane, I'm sure you've figured that out." They both laughed, and Rose left.

As she began unpacking her few items, she noticed that Rose had put a hook in the ceiling to hold the hanging plant. She got down on her knees and thanked God that he had brought her to this place. Thinking of her blessings, she began to cry. She stood up and finished unpacking. The room had no closet, as the guest house was built in the 1800s, but it did have a dresser and a wardrobe, plenty room enough to hold her few items. She carefully set the photograph of her two boys on the dresser, hoping that now she was settled her husband might agree to let her see them. They were eight and ten the last time she saw them. They'd be thirteen and fifteen now. Her heart ached when she thought of them.

She walked back up to the house and knocked on the door. Chloe answered. "Mr. MacKenzie asked me to come and see him. Is he available now?" Pamela inquired.

"He's in his office. Let me check." She came back and said Alex was ready to see her now. Pamela walked in, her knees shaking. She didn't know what to expect. Alex offered her a chair and closed the French doors.

"I wanted us to agree on a few essential items. I've had a contract drawn up," he said as he handed her a copy. "As you'll see, the contract can be revoked at any time I deem fit."

"I see."

"You can live in the guest house rent free for a period of one year. Food will be provided. You can either eat what Heidi and Chloe fix, or you can prepare your own meals in the guest house. It's up to you." He sounded stern, like he wasn't altogether happy with the arrangement.

"Mr. MacKenzie, if you don't really want me here, I'm sure Pastor Hartgrove can make other arrangements for me."

"It's not that I don't want you here. But I have to protect myself and my property. After all, you are a convicted felon." This didn't hit Pamela as hard as one would have expected. She had come to terms with that ugly fact long ago. "You'll earn $40 a week working in the garden you'll plant and helping Heidi and Chloe around here."

"That's more than I ever expected. I promise I won't disappoint you."

"I don't think you will. Now, about your business. I'll give you two acres for the first year. I'll bring in some of the guys from the orchard to lay sprinklers and prepare the ground for planting. After that, you're on your own. I'll provide the soil, mulch, seeds, tools, and anything else needed to get you started. I don't suppose you'll earn any money off of it the first year, but if you do, you can keep it. After the first year, a year from today's date, if it looks like it's gonna be a go we'll renegotiate the terms. If you're going to run a business from my ranch, I'll expect a share in the revenue."

"I don't know what to say. I've never experienced such generosity. I really don't know what to say."

"Heidi and Chloe will be glad to have the help."

"I won't let you down, Mr. MacKenzie. I'll make a go of the business. I know I will." They both signed on the bottom line, then Alex stood up to signal the meeting was over.

"You let me know what you need, Pamela. I'm in your court."

Pamela left, her eyes brimming with tears. She didn't want to talk to anyone just then, so she let herself out the front door and walked back down the lane. As she approached the guest house, Lee came up the lane in a truck. When he saw her, he pulled to a stop. "You ok?"

"Yes, yes, I am," she told him as he got out of the truck.

"You don't look ok."

"It's just all so much. So many blessings being bestowed on me at once. I don't know what to do with my feelings. I'm so fortunate, and I feel so undeserving, and I'm scared."

"Scared? What are you scared of?"

"I'm afraid I'll let everyone down."

"Well it seems to me you would be the one in control of that. You're not gonna let anybody down. You've got a lot of people around here pulling for you, Pamela. Including me. Don't you forget that." He opened the door to the guest house and stepped aside as she went in. "You come find me if you need any help, ok?" She nodded. He closed the door and left.

Chapter 29

September 7
Feminists protest the Miss America Pageant in Atlantic City, New Jersey.

September 9
Arthur Ashe wins the U.S. Open, becoming the first black man to win a Grand Slam tennis tournament.

I can kind of see what they mean," declared Rose as she and Alex were sitting in the living room watching the pageant. The broadcast of the beauty contest included flashes of the protests taking place outside. Women were throwing feminine products, like bras, pots and pans, false eyelashes, and other items into a "freedom trash can."

"Oh for crying out loud, Rose. It's been going on for almost 50 years. Who are they hurting?"

"I don't know. I'm just saying, I get what the feminists are thinking. These women are putting everything they have into their looks. Maybe there's something more important they could be doing. Oh, isn't she pretty!" she added as Miss New Mexico strutted across the stage.

Alex started laughing. "You really are my little hypocrite, aren't you?" he said as he took another swig of beer.

"Please get your feet off the table."

Alex and Rose had discussed their wedding but hadn't come up with a date yet. Rose was intent on having a Christmas party and wanted to get that behind them before they planned a wedding. They were tentatively thinking about next summer.

In the meantime, she began making plans for the Christmas party. They set the date for Friday, December 13. She started to draw up a guest list, including her extended family and some, but not all, of her friends. She didn't want to be responsible for anyone sneaking outside to smoke a joint. She included the people whom she had worked with at the museum. Alex's list was about twice as long as hers was. His included the managers and upper staff of all his enterprises: orchards, cattle, horses, oil, skin care products, stocks, and other endeavors Rose hadn't even been aware of.

The out-of-town guests would stay in the nineteen guest rooms; her parents would get the largest one at the top of the stairs. Perusing the list, she realized that there would be more than nineteen out-of-towners, so she asked Alex if she might call the Riverside Mission Inn and reserve several rooms there. He thought it was a good idea.

She wondered if she should hire a decorator the way Dede had, but decided against it. She wanted to do it herself. She sat down with Heidi, Chloe, and Pamela to draft some preliminary plans. She told them that she'd like the three of them to prepare the rooms, but she would hire a catering service to prepare and serve the food and a maid service to come in the following day and help with the clean-up. Although it was only September, the four women were excited about the upcoming holidays.

Mr. MacKenzie, may I please talk to you?" Pamela was nervous about approaching Alex, and usually tried to stay out of his way. He intimidated her. He was tall, dark, incredibly handsome, wealthy, and powerful. She felt unsophisticated around him, small. She found him as he was walking down the lane, past the guest houses toward the corral.

"Sure. Can you walk with me?"

She caught up with him but had to walk fast to keep up with him. She found herself talking fast too and made an effort to slow down her speech. "I was wondering if, when the men start laying the sprinklers, if maybe they could lay some around the perimeter of the house too. I think I could grow some impressive flower beds."

"What, you don't like the shrubbery?"

"Oh, of course I do, but..." He cut her off.

"I'm kidding. You know, flowers are the one thing this house has never had. It's always just been green shrubs, and I have to admit they're pretty old and woody. Sure, I'll have water lines laid. You'll have to let the guys know what kind of heads you want on them."

"Oh Mr. MacKenzie, thank you! It'll be beautiful, I swear it will be!"

"Can you sketch up your plans, so I know what I'm getting into?"

"Absolutely! I think you'll really like it! Of course, I can't even begin to plant until early spring. Except for the bulbs. I'd like to get them in pretty soon."

She went back to the studio and began to plan. After about an hour, Rose came in. She set up a canvas and began to paint as Pamela described her design. She would begin with just the flower beds in front of the house, which faced west and spanned the entire width of the house. To begin with, she would need to construct a lattice-work screen from the bottom of the porch to the ground. This would hide the underneath of the porch, which was always in shadow and where she knew no plants would grow. On it, honeysuckle and star jasmine vines would intertwine as they grew up the lattice screen and continued up to the railing that surrounded the porch.

These two vines would offer the homeowners and their guests a sweet aroma as they approached the front door. The vines would make up the fourth level of her four-level design. Level three would include large plants, mostly perennials, and be planted just in front of the vines. Here, Pamela planned to use blue hydrangeas, bushes of St. John's wort, and yellow English rose. The next level would be made up of plants that grew one to three feet in height. For this level she planned to intersperse lavender bushes with red dahlias, pink phlox, yellow ragwort, and blue violet lupines. Level one would be mostly annuals and groundcover. For this she liked Dusty Miller, poppies, anemones, and pansies. She'd like to plant English ivy as a ground cover to run through all of level one, but she knew it would take constant care so as not to choke out all the other plants. She decided to do it.

"And Rose, don't you think we should put in a lawn?"

"Absolutely!" So they added an acre of green in front of the house and around the sides. They also added a macadam drive coming in from the road. Rose created an impressionistic rendering of the design, and when it was complete the two women stood back and admired their work.

"It's gorgeous!" proclaimed Rose.

"I just hope Alex will like it," Pamela answered.

"How could he not?" demanded Rose. As soon as the paint was dry enough, they carried the painting up to the house and set it on the mantle above the fireplace. As expected, when Alex came in that afternoon he was amazed and more than pleased with what Pamela had designed and how artistically Rose had painted it. Work would begin after Christmas.

The two girls were at work in the kitchen while Pamela was busy cleaning the living room when a thunderous roar was heard outside. They all rushed to open the door to see what it was. Rose and Alex, who had been in his office, joined them. They opened the door to see Lee stepping out of a brand new Mustang. And this wasn't just any Mustang; it was a GT California Special, dark green in color. "Whoa, buddy!" exclaimed Alex. "What do you have there?"

"Limited edition, my friend. Made special for California!" Known as a Mustang GT/CS, the California Special had been created from a Shelby design and included features exclusive to the limited-edition model: fog lights, side scoops, rear spoiler, and side stripes with the GT/CS logo. Lee explained that this one didn't have the standard small-block engine, but a Cobra Jet 428; hence, the loud roar as he pulled up.

"Pammy, hop in and I'll take you for a spin!"

"What? Oh, but I have to..."

In unison, Chloe, Heidi, and Rose all yelled, "Go!"

So Lee opened the passenger side door and Pamela, somewhat tentatively, got in. Lee hopped into the driver's seat, fired up his new hot rod, and off they went. The three girls and Alex looked at each other in amazement, and Alex said simply, "Wow."

Chapter 30

September 24
CBS-TV's "60 Minutes" debuts.

The Christmas party was a little over two months away, and Rose was already getting nervous about the plans. Where would she get nineteen small Christmas trees? How would she decorate the large tree that would be placed next to the piano? And where would she get all the decorations for all these trees? Christmas decorations wouldn't even be available in the stores for another month, at least. To ease her mind, she went out to the studio to paint. Maybe she'd get some inspiration.

As had become her habit, Rose knocked a couple of times before letting herself in. She found Pamela at the big table sketching out some plans for the two acres but glad for the distraction. "There's so much to consider when you start with a blank slate," she confessed to Rose. "I'm not even sure where to begin."

"Tell me about it," responded Rose. "I'm feeling the same way about the party. I thought maybe by coming into my creative space I might get some inspiration." The two women sat across from each other, sharing looks of anxiety. "Maybe we can help each other."

"Maybe so. Let's talk about the party. The two acres are overwhelming me right now, but I think I can help you with your decorating ideas. Tell me what you're planning so far."

"Well, I want a large tree, a very large tree, in the corner by the piano. Then I want every guest room to have a small tree, maybe two or three feet tall. And I was thinking it would be nice to have a small gift bag under each tree for the guests. You know, maybe with some Camille Beckman products and a couple of other mementos? Of course, we'd also have bags to hand to the people who aren't staying at the house."

"Wow. How nice! Rose, aren't you ever concerned about cost? This party is going to cost you a fortune!"

"I know. I figure I'll just keep doing what I want until Alex brings the hammer down. So far he hasn't said a thing. Hasn't so much as even hinted about the cost." Then, as it dawned on her, she added, "I'm sorry, Pamela. That was very insensitive of me."

"Don't even say that, Rose! I wasn't thinking anything negative at all. If I was thinking anything, it was how life brings different fortunes to different people. At the moment, I feel like the luckiest woman alive."

"You're kind to let me off the hook. It really was insensitive. Besides, Alex owns half of the Camille Beckman business, so we'll save some money there." Then, making direct eye contact with Pam, she added, "I'm so glad our paths crossed. I feel like you're the good friend I never had."

Pamela got up from her high stool and gave Rose a big hug. "That's the most beautiful thing anyone has said to me in years. And I feel the same way about you. Are you going to decorate the outdoors as well as the indoors?"

"Ack! I hadn't even got that far. I suppose so."

"Think about poinsettias. They're so colorful. We could put pots of them on the steps and the porch. And lights. Do you think we could outline the whole house in colored lights?"

They sat there for a couple of hours coming up with one idea after another. Later that evening, when she shared her plans with Alex, she told him that her one big problem was that all of this would have to be done in the month of November, because the stores wouldn't be setting out their holiday products until then. He allayed her fears by assuring her that he could put as many crew members as necessary toward her jobs. That helped, but she still worried about all the last-minute shopping.

Chapter 31

September 30
*Boeing rolls out the 747 Jumbo Jet, the biggest
passenger plane the world has seen to date – 231 feet
long, wings spanning 196 feet and seats for 490.*

The Santa Ana winds were blowing. Satan. Santana.
Devil Winds. Or were they named for Saint Ana? No
one really knew, but what everyone could agree on was
that they brought trouble. Some even said crime went up
when they blew. On this day, they had started around
2:00 in the afternoon, warm, dry, and strong, blowing
from the northeast. No one was sure if the fire was
started by a car's backfire, kids target shooting, or a
careless match discarded into a dry shrub. Whatever
reason, a fire had started west of Riverside, and within
minutes it was blazing out of control.

"Looks like it's getting closer," Alex, concerned,
declared. He was standing on the upper deck that

spanned the south side of the upper level of the house, binoculars in hand, looking east. "I'm thinking we oughta start moving the cattle and horses out of here."

"I don't know. Why don't we watch it for a while longer?" Lee knew how quickly a fire could spread, but he also knew what a huge undertaking it would be to move the livestock.

"OK, awhile longer. But let's start bringing the trucks and trailers around."

Rose walked out the glass door of their bedroom and walked around the deck to where Alex was standing. "Surely they'll get it out before it gets close to us, Alex. I can see the water-dropping planes from here."

"Let's hope. I've gotta go help Lee with the trailers." He gave her the binoculars and left. Rose, who grew up in Placentia and now lived at the beach, was unaccustomed to wildfires. She found it somewhat frightening, but oddly mesmerizing.

An hour later, the local news reported that the fire was 0% contained. They didn't need binoculars to see the fire was creeping closer to the ranch.

Lee put Nick in charge of rounding up the cattle drivers, who would lead the 1000 head of cattle as far west as possible onto government land. Gustavos, who managed the orchards, called out all his workers and stationed them at intervals with water hoses. A large water tanker was kept on a flatbed truck, always ready for this purpose. Lee and Alex and enough others to man the six trucks and horse trailers took charge of moving the 24 Mustangs which they had recently brought down from Wyoming.

Another hour passed, and Alex told Rose to take Fitz and CaliCat and go to her own place in Laguna Beach, that he'd call her when he knew more. She didn't argue, because she could see for herself how close the flames were to their property. Truthfully, she was frightened and glad to be going, but she worried for the men working the ranch as well as for the house and property. Mac sent Heidi, Chloe, and Pamela to a hotel to wait out the danger.

The fire crews worked steadily throughout the late afternoon and into the night. By 11:00 the eastern rows of the orchard were on fire. The county firefighters and Gustavos' men fought brilliantly, but by morning all but about 100 of the 10,000 acres of orange trees had been destroyed. The charred remains stood like ghostly silhouettes reaching for the heavens, begging to be spared. The grazing land and the house had been saved.

Rose returned two days later to find Alex once again standing on the upper deck, looking east at the devastation. As she walked up to him, she tentatively asked, "What are you thinking?"

"Well, the house is still here. We'll be able to bring the cattle and horses back."

Dare she mention the orchard? "Alex, I'm so sorry. I have no idea what to say." She had no reference for normal in this situation. "Will you replant the oranges?"

He put his arm around her. "There's not a lot you can say, honey. And I don't know what I'm going to do."

Chapter 32

October 16
At the Olympic Games in Mexico City, Americans Tommie Smith and John Carlos receive the gold and bronze medals in the 200-meter dash, then raise gloved fists during the national anthem to protest violence toward and poverty among African-Americans. The next day, the International Olympic Committee strips their medals and sends them home.

It had been two weeks since the fire. The horses and cattle had returned home, but there was a lingering stench of charred death that wafted toward the house. Alex told Rose to continue to plan for the Christmas Party, that he thought they needed it more now than ever. She was amazed at his resilience. He had lost almost 10,000 acres of citrus but, after the first few days, had seemed to be OK. "Have you decided what to do about the orange groves?" she asked him.

"Not really. Thinking about it, though."

In Riverside, as she was driving to the halfway house to teach a class, she passed an empty lot with a sign that said, "Christmas Trees. Now Hiring." She pulled over and copied down the phone number. Later that day, once she had returned home, she dialed the number. A pleasant-sounding man answered the phone. She told him she had seen his sign on the vacant lot.

"You looking for work?" he inquired.

"No, I'm looking for nineteen small Christmas trees. I was hoping I could order them in advance." The deal was made, and she checked one item off her long list.

Hi, Charlie. Your secretary is so professional," commented Rose, when she finally got hold of her brother at his office. "But you haven't been available to take my call for several days."

"I know, Rose. I'm sorry about that. I've been swamped. What can I do for you?"

"I'd like you to help one of my friends."

"Does she have a lot of money? We're not cheap here, you know."

"No, actually she doesn't have any money. She just got out of a half-way house after being in prison for three years. She's staying with us until she can get on her feet."

"Ugh, Rose. How do you always find these degenerates?"

"She's not a degenerate, Charlie! She's a nice lady who fell on hard times and made a couple of bad decisions. It happens, you know." Rose filled him in on the details of Pamela's marriage, how she lost everything, including her sons, and how she ended up in prison.

"Well, it doesn't sound like a case that I could get reversed. What is she looking for?"

"She's not looking for anything. I am. And I don't need to get anything reversed, except for the restraining order that prevents her from seeing her sons. I have the name of her husband, if that would help."

"You know there are legal aid firms that could help her, don't you?"

"Yes, but your firm is so prestigious and well known. I think if her husband received a letter from you it would make much more of an impact on him."

"Can she pay on a sliding scale?"

"I doubt it. She only has the $40 a week that we pay her. But I'm willing to pay for her legal expenses, if I have to."

"No, I don't want you to do that. Let me take it to the partners and see if it's something they'd be willing to take on pro bono. Give me a week, and I'll get back to you."

"Oh Charlie, you're wonderful! Thank you so much! Say hi to Celeste and the kids!"

"I will. You do the same with Alex."

Rose hadn't mentioned her plans to Pamela, because she didn't want to get her hopes up in the event it wouldn't be possible for her to see her sons. But she felt confident that Charlie could make that happen.

Work was progressing on the preparation for Pamela's two acres. The land had been cleared and the sprinkler pipes were being layed. She would plant bulbs as soon as the land was ready and begin the seedlings of various cut flowers in the late winter and early spring. She suggested to Rose and Alex that the old shrubbery around the house not be pulled out before the Christmas party, that instead they could be strung with colored lights.

Alex shared the plans with Robby, who would need to work with the electrician to install new outlets around the house and along the roofline for the lights that would outline the entire house, roofline, gables, eaves, and all corners. These outlets, along with the new air conditioning and other new outlets resulting from the renovations, would necessitate installing up to 100 circuit breakers, about half on each side of the house. Robby assured him it could be done, but it wouldn't be cheap.

Pamela would fill in between and in front of the shrubs with winter blooming plants, such as cyclamen, rhododendron, witch hazel, red camellia, and late-blooming white roses. In front of all of these she would plant a double row of pansies and violas. Pots of red poinsettias and pots of holly berry would line the steps leading up to the porch. It would be a stunning display of winter horticulture in Riverside County.

The next week Charlie called Rose with the good news that his firm would take on Pamela's case pro bono. "She'll need to come in and sign some documents to get the process started," he told Rose.

When Rose told Pamela, she sat down, speechless. "Rose, I don't know what to say. Could this really be happening?"

"Yes, it really is happening, Pamela. But there are no guarantees. Charlie says the courts always prefer to reunite children with their parents, so there's a good chance he can get the restraining order lifted. But as he said, no guarantees."

Chapter 33

November 5
Nixon wins the presidency, beating Humphrey by just 0.7
of the popular vote. Segregationist candidate George
Wallace carries five Southern states.

I'm not going to replant," declared Alex as they were having coffee in the living room. Simon and Garfunkle's album *Bookends*, Rose's birthday gift, was gently sounding out of the stereo and *A Hazy Shade of Winter* had just started to play. "I've spent the last several weeks meeting with my finance advisor, attorneys, land developers, and home builders. I'm going to subdivide it into parcels and build homes on one parcel at a time. We'll begin with parcels to accommodate 30 homes each and go from there. We're going to do it ourselves, Rose. It'll be a huge undertaking, but it's what I want to do."

"I don't know what to say, Alex. It's huge! But so exciting!" Rose realized Alex needed a new interest in life. Managing the ranch was routine to him, and from the time she met him, she sensed that he was bored with life. She also sensed he wasn't altogether unhappy when the orchards were destroyed. "I'm thrilled, and I want to be a part of it!"

"Well, what they do is they build what they call model homes. We're going to have five styles, 3-, 4-, and 5-bedrooms, one- and two-level homes. Your job will be to decorate the models, make them look inviting."

"I know all about model homes. They create them in the subdivisions that have been built on my parents' old property. I'll love that job! How fun!"

"We won't break ground until the Spring. There's a lot of planning and permits that need to happen first. I thought we'd call the development 'Orange Acres.' What do you think?"

"I think it's perfect, and I can't wait for it to begin!"

They celebrated Alex's 49th birthday the same way they had celebrated Rose's, quietly. She had bought him two Van Heusen shirts, one white with blue pinstripes and a white collar and cuffs, and the other one a dark rose color, which she hoped he would like. He said he did. "Especially this rose one, from my Rose." She bought him a pair of sunglasses that looked like the ones Steve

McQueen had worn in Bullet, the only movie she had been able to talk him into seeing that year. But he mostly liked his main gift. She had enlisted Lee to help her take one of his branding irons to a blacksmith. There, she had a miniature branding iron made, one that could be used to sear steaks grilling on the BBQ. "I have never seen anything like this!" he exclaimed. "You are so clever! We'll have to have a BBQ soon so I can try this baby out!" She was thrilled that she had pleased him.

Christmas decorations were beginning to appear in the stores, and Rose didn't waste any time beginning her purchases. The first thing she did was to buy nineteen sets of 10' colored lights, one each for the trees in each of the guest rooms. She bought six 20' lengths of clear lights for the tree that would be in the living room and another four 20' lengths of colored lights for the tree that would go in their bedroom.

She bought a box of one dozen colored bulb ornaments for each of the small trees, plus six individual ornaments for each tree. The bulbs for each tree would match the colors of the room, for instance, turquoise and rose bulbs would be placed on the trees in the rooms with that color scheme. The individual ornaments were a variety of shapes and sizes: stars, bells, Santa Clauses, reindeer, snowmen, and other holiday representations.

On this particular trip, she didn't buy much for the big tree in the living room, as she still wasn't quite sure what she was going to do with it. Dede had written that hers had an orange theme. What did that mean? Orange ornaments? Real oranges? But she did buy a dozen gold stars and a dozen gold bells for the tree, just in case.

When she got home, she unpacked the lights and ornaments, setting them in the rooms in which they'd be used. Then she turned her thoughts to the gift bags that would be set out for the guests in each room and handed to the guests who wouldn't be staying. She had asked Alex to have Camille contact her so she could put in the order. She was pleased to find out that Camille had called her that day while she was out, so she returned her call.

Camille suggested that she send Rose a list of all their products, showing which products were available in which scents. She told Rose she would only need a few days to fill the order. Between the tree decorations and the plans for the gift bags, Rose's stomach was filled with butterflies. She was so excited about the party preparations, but at the same time she was very anxious that all would go well. But it was more than just anxiety. Lately she was feeling nauseous, particularly in the mornings.

Chapter 34

November 9
Yale University, after 267 years, decides to admit female undergraduates, beginning in 1969.

I knew this was going to happen," complained Alex. "I knew once Yale did this the other ivy leaguers would do the same thing. Now my alma mater has decided to admit women next Fall. You wait and see. Soon Dartmouth, Columbia, all of them will do the same thing. Heck, even Harvard will eventually merge with Radcliffe. You mark my words."

Rose thought it was a wonderful breakthrough. "I don't understand how you can be so unwilling to change, Alex. You're so old-school." She laughed at her pun, but Alex didn't think it was funny. She went up to him and put her arms around his neck. "The world isn't going to end, honey. As a matter of fact, it will be better because more educated women will be contributing to it."

Heidi, Chloe, and Pamela looked at each other and rolled their eyes, but none of them was about to enter into the conversation. Until Chloe chimed in, "Your age is showing, Mr. MacKenzie." And then everyone laughed. Alex acknowledged she was probably right, then left them to their gift bags.

The Camille Beckman products had arrived, and the four women sat at the dining room table assembling them. Rose had bought the gift bags in colors to match the décor of the rooms.

The invitations had gone out and most of the replies had come in. For couples, larger bags would be used to hold products for both men and women. For their single guests, the bags would hold either women's or men's products.

For the women, Rose had chosen four scents: English Lavender, French Vanilla, Glycerine Rosewater, and Gardenia Breeze. All of the men's products would come from the Oriental Spice collection.

Gift bags with the English Lavender scent held a jar of glycerine hand therapy, silky body cream, a bar of soap, and a bottle of bubble bath. The bags with the French Vanilla scent held the glycerine hand therapy, bubble bath, perfumed body powder, and Eau de Parfum. The guests who would receive gifts from the Rosewater collection would get a jar of glycerine hand therapy, silky body cream, a bar of soap, and a bottle of fragrant body mist. The bags containing the products from the Gardenia Breeze collection included glycerine hand therapy, silky body cream, a bar of soap, and a bottle of fragrant body mist. The men's products included glycerine hand therapy, cleansing gel, and a bar of soap.

Every bag also included a bag of pistachios, and a bag of dates, both locally grown in Riverside County, and a $40 gift card to Glen Ivy Hotel and Hot Springs in nearby San Bernardino County. All of the bags also included a bar of soap from the Orange Crème fragrance collection. Rose had considered filling all gift bags from this collection but thought it might be overkill on the orange theme. In the end, she added a bar of soap as a token orange product. Once a sheet of colored tissue paper was stuffed into the top of each bag and name tags attached, Rose proclaimed the job to be done. There were plenty of extra products to fill bags for the people who hadn't yet responded, or for people who showed up without responding at all.

The women celebrated the completion of the job with glasses of wine, which Heidi and Chloe brought into the living room with a platter of cheeses and crackers. Aretha Franklin's album, *I Never Loved a Man the Way I Love You*, was on the stereo and the women sang along to *RESPECT,* celebrating the fact that they were women. Eventually Heidi said she and Chloe had to start dinner and Pamela said she would clean up the gift bags and set the table.

Rose went upstairs, where soon Alex joined her and showed her just how much he respected her. "Rose, my lovely lady, I do believe your breasts are getting larger."

"Do you think I'm putting on weight?"

"I haven't noticed that you have. It's just your breasts. And, I might add, they're beautiful."

I'm so nervous I think I'm going to be sick."

"Just take deep breaths," Rose advised. "You'll be fine."

Charlie had been able to get the restraining order against Pamela lifted, and now she and Rose sat on the patio of a small French restaurant in downtown Riverside. They were waiting for the court-appointed supervisor to arrive, followed by Pamela's two sons, Larry and Bobby. It had been five years since she had seen them. They were now teenagers. What would she say to them? What had their father told them about her?

The supervisor arrived and explained the details of the meeting. The meeting was scheduled to last for 45 minutes. If any of the participants wanted to end it before then, but another participant wanted to continue, the meeting would continue as planned. The boys' father, Stephen, could sit in on the meeting if he so desired.

They walked in, Stephen, Larry, and Bobby. Pamela was so nervous that when she stood to greet them, she knocked over her chair, but before it crashed to the ground Rose stuck out her hand and caught it. Pamela, Stephen, and the boys just stood there, looking at each other. The supervisor broke the ice. "Why don't you two boys sit here across from your mother? Mr. Caldwell, are you going to stay for the meeting?"

"Yes, yes I will." Before anyone else could say anything, a waiter appeared to take their orders. "We're not going to be here that long," Stephen informed him. "Maybe we can see your dessert menu?" The boys ordered root beer floats while the adults just had coffee. Pamela couldn't take her eyes off her sons.

"You've grown so much! You're so handsome! Please, tell me what you've been up to these last few years. Bobby, do you still like model planes?"

"It's Bob."

"What? Oh, of course. Bob." Rose surreptitiously put her hand under the table and patted Pamela's knee for assurance.

"He doesn't like model planes anymore," answered Larry.

"Oh, well then, what does he like to do now? And you, Larry. What do you like?"

The boys looked at their father, as if seeking permission to speak to this woman. "Go ahead, boys. Answer her question."

Larry went first. "I like to skateboard, mostly. I've tried surfing and I really like it. Next year when I get my license Dad says I can drive myself to the beach. Maybe even in the morning before school. That's when the surf's the best."

"Wow! Driving! Do you have your permit?" Pamela was starting to get into the flow of the conversation.

"Just last week. Got a 98% on my written test!"

"You always were a smart one, Larry." Larry smiled and shrugged, and Pamela gazed at him as though she were seeing the past five years come and go before her eyes. "What about you, Bobby. I mean, Bob. Do you like to skateboard too?"

"Not really."

"Bob's more studious, Pamela. Perhaps you've forgotten that," Stephen admonished.

Pamela's heart sank at the rude reminder that she'd been out of their lives for so long. "No, no I haven't forgotten." She smiled as she made eye contact with Bobby, or Bob. "You used to love looking at bugs, but I supposed you've graduated from them by now."

Larry laughed. "Not much!" Bob gave him a playful punch in the arm.

"I actually still like insects. I like studying biology."

"I like botany," Pamela offered enthusiastically. "As a matter of fact, I'm starting a business. I'll be growing flowers to sell to local businesses and residences. Of course, it'll take a few years to get off the ground, but I've at least started."

"Where'd you get the money to do that?" questioned Stephen.

Before Pamela could answer, Rose cut in. "Pamela and Mr. MacKenzie have gone into the business together. Pamela is the brains behind it."

"That's a shocker. And you didn't have to put up any money? Sounds like a great start to a losing business."

Rose thought she saw disappointment in the boys' faces. She hoped it was for their father's rudeness, and not for their mother.

"I, uh," but Pamela had no answer to his derision.

"Mr. MacKenzie wouldn't invest in a losing business, Mr. Caldwell. He has great confidence in Pamela's knowledge and ability."

"Well, it's just about been 45 minutes," broke in the supervisor. "I'll call each of you this week to see if you'd like to schedule a follow-up meeting, or not."

On the drive home, Rose offered her opinion. "He's awful."

"Yes, he is. But weren't the boys wonderful? I can't believe how much they've grown and how handsome they are!"

"That, they are! And they didn't seem all that awkward around you. Will you see them again?"

"If it's up to me, definitely. I hope Stephen will agree."

"He's threatened by you, Pamela. It was obvious the boys were happy to see you. And now you're a budding businesswoman, pardon my pun." They both laughed. "And you're beautiful and you're gaining confidence in yourself. He's gonna regret that he ever lost you."

"He didn't lose me. He threw me out."

"Well, whatever. He's gonna regret it. Pamela, if he agrees to it, would you like to invite them to our Christmas party?"

"I would love to have the boys there! But Stephen would never allow them to come on their own. Nor, I doubt, would the supervisor."

"Then let's invite them all! Not to stay at the house, of course. They can either stay at the Mission

Inn or drive home that night." So it was decided that when the supervisor called, Pamela would run the idea by him. The thought of seeing Missy, Stephen's wife and legal partner and the woman who broke up their marriage, was intimidating. Maybe she wouldn't come.

Chapter 35

November 12
The Supreme Court unanimously rules that an Arkansas law prohibiting the teaching of evolution in public schools violates the First Amendment.

Rose walked out of the OB-GYN's office feeling like she was floating on air. She hadn't had her period in two months, not that she thought Alex had noticed. But the nausea, enlarged breasts, and recent changes in her waistline made it pretty obvious to her what was going on.

But as she drove home, a sobering thought hit her. What if Alex didn't want a baby? They had never discussed the subject. He was 48 years old. Maybe he would think he was too old.

At some point they had quit using protection. Surely he knew the consequences. But men could be fickle. Maybe he assumed that was her responsibility, but she hadn't been doing anything to prevent a pregnancy, just as he hadn't. She could raise the baby alone. Her parents would help her. She didn't need Alex, if that's the way he was going to be. Thinking about his possible rejection, she began to cry. How was she going to tell him? She had made the doctor's appointment for the same day as her art class at the half-way house, so Alex didn't know anything about it. He would probably be out at the corral and not even realize that she was coming home later than usual. After a few minutes, she dried her tears and tried to focus on her driving.

Next week they would be attending the Autumn Gala at the MacKenzie Museum of Local History. The museum board had decided that to honor the agriculture industry that had put Riverside on the map, they would hold their annual fundraising gala in the fall, to celebrate the harvest.

"Will we really be taking your truck to the gala?" Rose asked Alex with a note of despair.

"Well, I'm certainly not driving that little toy you drive."

"Excuse me, but my Porsche is a beautiful car, one that anyone would be proud to own!"

"Right. A little small, for my taste. I was actually thinking about getting a new car, a sedan."

"Really? What a great idea! Do you think we could get it before the gala so we could go in style?"

That weekend they went car shopping. "Where will we go first?" asked Rose.

"I don't know. I was thinking of looking at the Buicks. They've got nice lines this year."

"OK. I was thinking about a Mercedes."

"No, I want to buy an American car."

"Of course you do."

So they began at the Buick dealership. Alex was drawn to the Rivieras. He liked the V8, 365 horsepower engine with the turbo automatic transmission. The green metallic one Rose liked had air conditioning and came with a radio. She was ready to drive off the lot with it, but Alex suggested they look at Cadillacs too.

At the Cadillac dealership, they looked at a 2-door Coupe de Ville. They agreed to test-drive a red one with a white convertible top. This one had a 375 horsepower V8 engine with an automatic transmission. It also came with power windows, air conditioning, and a radio. The wheels had chrome spokes and whitewall tires.

As they were returning to the lot, Rose declared, "I love this car!"

"I knew you would. It's Rose Red."

But Rose wasn't thinking about the color. She was thinking that a baby's car seat would fit over the front seat in this car better than it would in the Porsche.

"You want to go over and see the Oldsmobiles? The new Cutlasses look nice."

"I don't think so. I think I want this one, if it's ok with you."

"Whatever you want, imp."

Alex suggested Rose drive the Coupe de Ville home, and he would drive the truck. He also suggested they put the convertible top back on until she got used to driving the car. After all, it was at least twice the size of her Porsche.

As she drove, she listened to the radio, KRLA AM 1110. DJ Casey Kasem was playing *The Look of Love* by Sergio Mendes. She was envisioning driving down the road with a baby in the car seat next to her. Perhaps, if Alex said he didn't want her or the baby, she could ask him if she could keep the car. He at least owed her that, didn't he?

Chapter 36

November 26
O.J. Simpson of USC wins the Heisman Trophy.

The man from the tree lot called informing her that the
lot would open for business next week and that her
nineteen small trees and two large ones would be ready
then. The next week, Rose rode in the truck with Nick
to pick up the trees. When they returned, the girls came
out of the house and helped unload the small trees, while
Nick carried one large tree into the living room and the
other large one up to their bedroom. She had purchased
water containers for all the trees and those were brought
in too. Alex showed up later and helped Nick to set the
two large trees into their containers, straighten and
stabilize them, and string the lights on them.

Rose and the girls got right to work with the
decorations. As Heidi, Chloe, and Pamela worked on the
nineteen small trees, Rose decorated the tree in their

bedroom. Since the lights were already on it, it wasn't a lot of work to add the other decorations. Then, she spent about an hour carefully draping the individual pieces of tinsel over the needles of the Douglas fir. She stepped back to admire it. It was so beautiful standing in the corner between the fireplace and the door to the outside deck. Tonight they would turn on the lights and their bedroom would look magical.

She went downstairs and stood in front of the large tree in the living room. For this, she had chosen all clear light bulbs, but she still didn't know how it would be decorated. What did Dede mean when she said it had an orange theme? Just then Alex came in carrying three dusty boxes. "Look what I found out in the garage." He opened one of the boxes to reveal a dozen hand-blown glass ornaments, all molded to look like oranges. Each one was three inches in diameter.

"What? Alex, they're beautiful! What are in the other two boxes?" Alex took the lids off the other two boxes to find two dozen more orange ornaments. "Alex, I can't believe this! They're glass oranges! Did you know you had them?"

"No, but I knew my dad had stored some old boxes up in the rafters of the garage, and I wondered if the ornaments might be up there. So, imp, here are your oranges."

Rose was excited to start hanging the three dozen glass oranges. The oranges were the main theme, but they weren't the only ornaments on the tree. Considering the fact that they no longer actually had orange groves, she didn't want to overdo it with orange bows or all orange lights. So among these beautiful ornaments she also hung the gold stars and bells. By the time she was finished, the sun was going down. She called Alex in so they could witness the tree together as they plugged in the lights. It was magical. The clear light bulbs lit up, shining their light through the hand-blown glass. As the lights heated up, their heat waves danced among the bells, adding a faint ringing sound to the room. Even Alex was speechless. Instead of commenting, he pulled Rose close to him and gave her a beautiful, sensuous kiss. About that same time, the girls came downstairs and were awed by the beauty of the tree. Rose went over to the stereo and put on a Christmas album while the girls assisted her in placing long boughs of pine on the mantle. Alex helped to intertwine lights through the boughs.

Later that night, Rose turned on the lights on the tree in their bedroom. Alex told her he had some turning on of his own to do.

The next night was the gala. As Alex finished adjusting his cummerbund, he turned to see Rose standing in front of the tree, a fire burning in the fireplace. There were no other lights lit in the room. His breath caught in his throat. Rose stood there, seeming to glow. She had on a shear white dress that shone with some kind of iridescence. Silver threads, embroidered around a high collar and the hemline, added to the glimmer. It was gathered lightly from the neckline and hung loose to just above her knees. It had no sleeves. She was wearing white shimmery nylons and silver high heels. Her hair was down, hanging straight to her waist except for a silver comb holding one side of her hair up over her ear. He was stunned, thinking he'd never seen such a beautiful sight in all his life.

"Rose," he whispered.

"Alex, I have something to tell you," she said in her own whispered voice.

"No, don't talk. I just want to look at you. You are the most beautiful apparition I've ever seen."

She stood there for a minute, growing more and more nervous about sharing her news with him. "I'm going to have a baby."

Alex couldn't speak. He couldn't move. It was, after all these years, a revelation to him. He now knew why his father loved his mother. And how much. Tears welled in his eyes, and he still couldn't speak. Finally, Rose's next words brought him back to earth.

"You're shocked, I can see. I know this wasn't what we planned, and I won't blame you if you don't want it, I mean, I can go live with my mother until I have the baby and..."

"Rose! What are you talking about?" He went to her and held her in his arms. "It's just, well, I was entranced by your beauty, you standing there in the glow of the tree, and now you tell me we're bringing a new life into this world? My God, Rose, I'm the happiest man in the world! You have never been more beautiful, and I have never felt such love as I feel for you right now."

He walked her over to the loveseat and sat down with her. "When? How long have you known? Are you ok? Do we need to see a doctor? Would you rather not go tonight?"

Rose laughed. "I suspected it about three weeks ago, and I saw the doctor two weeks ago. I'm about three months along, so the baby is due in May. I'm feeling fine, kind of queasy in the mornings but he said that should pass soon." All of a sudden she began to cry, and then he did too. They laughed and cried together.

"Does anybody else know? Your mom? Pamela?"

"Of course not! I would never have told anyone before telling you. Oh Alex, I was so nervous to tell you, so worried about how you would respond."

"Honey, how could you have doubted me? You know I love you. And I'm no idiot. I knew what could happen when I quit wearing the condoms." At that they laughed again. "Do you want to go tonight, or would you rather stay home?"

"I want to go on the arm of the man I love."

On the drive over to the museum, Alex said, "Maybe we shouldn't wait until summer to get married."

"No, no probably not. When do you want to do it?"

"The sooner the better with me. How about the week after Christmas?"

"Really? That soon?"

"Yes. I don't want you changing your mind on me."

The museum board had hired a valet service for the gala. Alex was proud to pull up in front in their brand new Cadillac with the most beautiful woman in the world beside him. As he got out of the car, the valet helped Rose out of the passenger seat.

They walked into the lobby, which looked the same as it had back in January. "I remember this room. It's where the buyer complained to me that the benefactor was a cheap bastard." Rose looked up at him and they both laughed.

"A lot has happened since that night, no?"

"Sure has, thank my lucky stars. There's your fake Georgia O'Keefe," he said, pointing at the picture that was the focal point of the room.

"You were sure right to buy a reproduction. All the school kids coming through here on field trips. Just thinking about their sticky little hands makes me cringe!"

A silent auction had been set up on tables lining the hallways of the museum. A huge tent had been set up outside for the dinner and live auction. Rose and Alex had donated many of the items for the silent auction, such as baskets of Camille Beckman products; half bushels of oranges with gold ribbon entwined to make them look festive and scrumptious; tickets to next year's Pageant of the Masters in Laguna; several pieces of pottery that Rose had made; and other items.

After they had made high bids on a number of other items, they found their way to the outdoor tent. They had been given a seat at the head table, and Alex was introduced as the founder and benefactor of the museum.

Following in his father's footsteps and in accordance with Dede's journals, for the live auction they offered a dinner for ten couples. Alex knew he'd have a lot of work to do up on the high plateau on the western edge of the ranch to get it ready for the dinner. But Rose was excited to help, and she had Dede's description of their dinners as reference. They didn't really need to worry about it right now, as the item was described to take place the following Fall. They thought that would insure them good weather, neither too hot nor too cold. Besides that, the guests of the very classy dinner would still be talking about it by the time the next gala rolled around, almost guaranteeing an even greater response.

That Thursday was Thanksgiving. They were all going to Charlie and Celeste's house for dinner. Alex was impressed with Charlie's girls, who were aged 10 and 13. They played hostess while their mother and two aunts made last-minute preparations. They took Rose's sweater and offered Alex a seat in the den with the other men. He got a kick out of them and wondered if he would be lucky enough to have a little girl. Rose's other brother, John, didn't have children. Alex never would have given it a second thought before, but now he felt sorry for John and his wife.

It was a beautiful, traditional Thanksgiving spread, and everyone ate until they were satiated. Then the men returned to the den to watch football while the women cleaned up the dinner. After about an hour, the men were called back to the table for dessert. Rose had told Alex on the drive over that she thought they should make their announcement during dessert. So once everyone was seated and the plates of pumpkin pie were passed around, Alex stood up.

Talking stopped while everyone looked at him. "I'm happy to tell you that Rose and I are moving up our wedding. We're going to get married the week after Christmas."

Everyone oohed and aahed and said how wonderful that was, as the reason for the earlier wedding dawned on them. Celeste was the first to speak. "Rose, are you...?"

"Yes, yes I am!" And the room exploded with excitement. "I'm due in May!" Edna got out of her chair and hugged her daughter. Her eyes glimmered with tears. Robert rose and proclaimed how happy they were that Alex would soon be a member of their family, shook his hand and gave Rose a kiss.

Chapter 37

December 3
Elvis Presley begins a comeback from years of torpor and schlock with a one-hour special on NBC-TV.

Pamela and Lee were strolling through the Main Street Pedestrian Mall in downtown Riverside. Pamela needed something to wear to the Christmas party next week. "I'm very nervous about Stephen and boys coming. And it looks like his wife will be coming too." She had already told Lee the story of her life, her marriage, divorce, arrest, and recent reacquaintance with her sons. Lee was always reassuring to her; she felt as though she had known him all her life. He seemed to be very interested in her, but so far their friendship was platonic. She felt no pressure from him to take it further.

"Do they know where you live? Do they know anything about the ranch?"

"I don't think so. Stephen and his wife are so snobby. I'm sure they think I'm living in a shack. And I doubt they know anything about the MacKenzie Ranch."

"Then they're in for a big surprise, aren't they?"

She found a pair of shiny, gold, hip-hugger, bell-bottom pants, that fit her thin build perfectly. She purchased a white satin blouse with peasant sleeves that gathered at the wrist with a 3-inch ruffle. Pamela had blond, shoulder-length hair that was naturally curly, so if she didn't iron it straight it coiled itself in loose curls. As a gift, Lee bought her a pair of gold hoop earrings. The outfit would be stunning on her.

The exterior of the house dressed up for Christmas was exquisite. Colored lights were strung on every ridge and eave of the house. Pamela had orchestrated the planting and lighting of the flower beds in front of the house, much to Rose's delight and Alex's satisfaction. Large, vibrant red poinsettias dominated the porch, where a huge Della Robia fruit wreath hung on the front door. A lighted Nativity scene was placed near the bottom of the steps, reminding everyone of the purpose of the season.

The caterers came out to inspect where they'd be working. Like everyone else who entered the house, they were taken by its grandeur. It was decided that they would arrive early in the afternoon on the day of the party and prepare the food in the kitchen, rather than preparing it off-site and transporting it. Six people would be working in the kitchen, while four others, dressed in matching wait uniforms, would circulate among the guests, bearing trays of hor d'oeuvres. Additionally, a meat chef would be set up in the dining room, cutting slices of prime rib, ham and turkey for guests who desired something heartier than snacks. A variety of soups and vegetables would be available in that area too. A large Christmas cake was set on the sideboard, which itself had been decked out in lights and tinsel.

The weather had been warm, especially for December. Today it was 75 degrees and the night of the party was expected to be in the high 60s. So the caterers suggested they set up tables and chairs on the first-floor deck in front of the house, alleviating overcrowding inside. These tables would be draped in red tablecloths and have holiday centerpieces.

Chapter 38

December 9
Douglas C. Englebart's 90-minute presentation at the Fall Joint Computer Conference in San Francisco includes the world's first mouse and word processor.

With only four days to go before the party, Rose discovered she had nothing to wear. Seemingly almost overnight, her body had changed, leaving her with no waistline and a small but growing bump in her abdomen. "What am I going to do?" she cried to her mother. "The dress I had planned to wear doesn't fit me now!"

"Why don't you come down here and I'll see what can be done. Maybe I can make you up something."

"Mom! The party is in four days! I can't leave!" She was near hysterics.

"Sure you can, honey. What more do you need to do?"

So that afternoon Rose drove to her parents' house in Placentia. The next morning she and her mom went shopping at the newly opened Fashion Island in Newport Beach. It had four department stores: The Broadway, Buffum's, Robinson's and Penney's. Rose lamented that the maternity clothes were all matronly. "Am I supposed to wear these things for the rest of my pregnancy? They're horrid!"

"I guess I'd better get sewing!"

"Yes, you'd better." They both laughed, then headed for the fabric store.

They chose a pattern with an empire waist, not a maternity pattern but one that was trendy and would still hide her changing body and be comfortable. The front of the pattern envelope depicted two options, knee-length and ankle-length. Rose told her mother that she wanted it to be a mini-dress. She decided on an emerald green velvet.

As soon as they got home, her mother laid out the fabric and cut out the pattern. Within an hour she started sewing. Rose fixed something for them to eat, knowing her father shouldn't miss a meal just because her mother was busy making her a new outfit. By 7:00 that evening, all that remained was the hem. Her mom suggested they do that in the morning, as she was tired from shopping and sewing. Rose realized how much she was asking of her mother. The fact that her mom was now 71 years old didn't elude her either. A year ago she may have expected this work from her mom; now she marveled at what her mother was willing to do for her. She went over and gave her mother a loving hug. "Of course, Mom. It's time to quit for tonight."

The next morning Rose awoke early and brought a breakfast tray to her mother, who was still in bed. "What's this?" exclaimed her mom.

"It's the least I can do for you, Mom. I can't believe how quickly you whipped up a new dress for me! I want you to know how very grateful I am."

"It's been fun, honey. I think I'd better leave the sewing machine set up if I'm expected to make you a whole new maternity wardrobe!"

"Oh, you don't have to, Mom. Maybe if I bought some of those ugly things we saw today and just made them shorter, I could get by."

"Nonsense. We'll make you some stylish clothes to last through your pregnancy. I don't know why maternity clothes haven't changed with the times. They look just like they did when I was pregnant with you!" This brought a laugh from Rose. "I think if we buy some maternity patterns and make them out of stylish fabric, it would be a big improvement."

"And make them shorter!" declared Rose, emphatically.

Rose stood while her mother pinned up the hemline on the green velvet dress. When Rose looked at it in the full-length mirror, she said, "I think I'd like it a little shorter. About ¾ up my thigh." It seemed awfully short to her mother, but Edna knew that was the trend now, and most people at the party wouldn't even know that Rose was pregnant, so no one would think it inappropriate. So the dress was hemmed to Rose's specification, ironed, and folded neatly into a box for the drive home.

The night of the party arrived. The caterers had been busy in the kitchen most of the day. In the early evening, all the lights had been turned on, both inside and outside. Rose's parents had arrived in the afternoon. They would be staying in the largest guest room, the one at the top of the stairs. Her mother was in awe of how beautiful the house was, especially dressed up in its Christmas finery. She hadn't been there since May, when it was still in the throes of renovation. Rose's father had never seen it before, so Alex drove him around the ranch for a couple of hours before it was time for them to get ready for the party.

Rose was dressed in her new velvet mini-dress. She wore white shimmery nylons with black patent leather platform shoes. Heidi had done her hair for her. She had teased the front of Rose's hair and used a hair pad to give extra height to the top of her head, pulling the front of the hair back and over the pad. She secured it under the pad with a white grosgrain bow, allowing the hair to hang low down her back. The result was alluring, long dark hair, emerald green velvet mini-dress, and high platform shoes. Rose was pleased with herself when she looked in the mirror. Alex was stunned. He never tired of looking at his beautiful, stylish, soon-to-be wife. "Shall we go down?" he asked. They descended the stairs together to await their guests.

Pamela and Lee were the first to arrive. Rose was awestruck by how beautiful Pamela looked, and she told her so. "Isn't she though?" Lee responded as he handed Pamela a cup of eggnog. Edna and Robert came down to join them, and before long the living room was overflowing with guests. Charlie and Celeste were there, along with John and his wife, Jackie. They would all be staying at the house. Heidi and Chloe, although guests themselves, escorted the guests who were staying upstairs to their rooms.

Stephen arrived with the boys. Missy was with him. Missy was wearing a black shift. Her hair was pulled back and twisted into a French roll. As Rose greeted them, she couldn't help but notice how severe Missy looked, especially compared to Pamela, whose loose blond curls gave her a softer, younger appearance. And compared to Missy's black shift, although it was attractive and appropriate for the occasion, Pamela looked stylish and hip. Her tight gold pants fit her like a glove. And Lee had added to her beauty with a Christmas corsage of white and red roses, baby's breath, greenery, and red, white and gold ribbons entwined through the flowers. The gold ribbon was shimmery to match her hip-hugger, bell-bottom pants. When she and Lee noticed the arrival, Lee offered her his arm and together they approached her ex-husband, his wife, and her sons. Alex, who had been mingling with other guests, saw who had just arrived and appeared at the door about the same time Pamela and Lee had. He shook hands with Stephen, then Lee did the same. "Welcome to the ranch," Alex offered, sounding truly gracious and hospitable.

Larry and Bobby, now Bob, were gazing into the room, their eyes wide and a look of amazement on both their faces. Stephen's and Missy's faces betrayed their own amazement. "Come in, come in. Get a drink! Boys, there's food in the dining room. There are also plenty of snacks around. Just grab some off one of the trays as it passes you," encouraged Alex. The boys didn't hesitate to enter the room and disappear into the crowd.

"Do you live here?" inquired Stephen of Pamela.

"I live in a guest house on the property," she answered, feeling much more comfortable now that she was on Lee's arm.

"Hmph. It's nice," he responded. Missy never said as much as hello. They moved past their hosts and into the room. Alex winked at Pamela and Rose stifled a laugh.

Later, Larry asked his mother the same question as Stephen had, if she lived here. Now, she offered to show the boys the guest house, so she and Lee escorted them down the lane to her house. She feared they would be very disappointed to see how small it was; quite the opposite, they seemed to be very impressed, especially with the kiln. Pamela and Lee had set up a small Christmas tree in the guest house, so Pamela turned on the lights, giving the little house a warm, comfortable ambiance. "Oh, here, these are for you," she said as she handed each of them several presents. "You can save them for Christmas morning if you'd rather," she offered. Bob informed her that they opened their gifts on Christmas Eve, a new tradition of which she hadn't been aware. Her face must have revealed her thoughts, because Lee quickly interjected, "Well maybe you could save these for Christmas morning. Something special from your mother." But all in all, conversation with her boys was easier than it was when she had met them at the restaurant, and soon they walked back up to the big house to resume the party. She suggested they set their presents under the tree until they were ready to leave.

By midnight about half the guests had departed and most of the others were starting to say good night. Some of the guests who were staying in the house had already gone upstairs. As people departed, Chloe and Rose made certain they each received their personalized gift bag. When they gave Missy hers, she seemed to accept it reluctantly, as though she wanted nothing to do with this hospitality. The truth is, she had never even thought to hand her guests something on their way out the door, and she parsimoniously thought it was a waste of money. But she took the bag and left.

By the time the last guest departed, and all their staying guests had gone upstairs, it was past 1:00 and Rose was exhausted. But Alex restarted one of the Christmas albums that had been playing throughout the night. When the stylus landed on the first song, *O Holy Night*, he took Rose into his arms for a meltingly slow dance. She placed her head on his chest and said, "I love you, Alex." He held her tightly. The next song was Wayne Newton's version of *Jingle Bell Rock*, and Alex twirled Rose around the living room in a peppy little dance. Then they sat down in their beautiful living room and quietly enjoyed the music and the tree. He lifted her face to his and said, "I love you, too. Merry Christmas, imp."

As they were crawling into bed, Alex asked, "What do you bet Lee didn't drive home tonight?"

"I hope not," answered Rose.

The guests who had spent the night were treated to a lovely breakfast spread prepared by Heidi and Chloe. The two girls seemingly never tired and had arrived at the house before anyone had emerged from their rooms. They served leftover ham, scrambled eggs, toast, and several vegetables left over from the night before. The meal was set out on the sideboard so the guests could help themselves as they pleased. The cleaning crew had also arrived very early. By the time the last of the guests had descended the stairs, the party mess had been cleared out of the living room and off the porch and was mostly relegated to the kitchen.

By 1:00 only Rose's family members remained. They were all seated in the living room. Even though it was mild outside, Alex lit the fireplace. "So," asked Charlie, "what are the plans for the wedding?"

Alex looked at Rose, seeming to toss the question to her. They had spoken to each other about their plans, but this was the first they'd be sharing them. "We're going to get married on December 30. It's a Monday."

"A Monday?" exclaimed Edna. "Will a priest allow that?"

"We're not going to get married in the Church, Mom. We can't, because you have to take marriage preparation classes, and we don't have time for that. Besides, neither of us really goes to church. But we're going to change that, right Alex?"

"That's the plan."

"Honey, I could probably call Father Sullivan and explain your situation. I'm sure he'd marry you," said Edna, hopefully.

"No, Mom. We're going to do it this way. After the baby comes, we plan to have the marriage blessed in the Church. And we'll definitely have the baby baptized Catholic!"

"Well, ok. Of course it's your decision." There was disappointment in Edna's statement.

"So are we going to have a party on Monday night?" asked Jackie, John's wife. "You could all come over to the house!"

Rose looked at Alex, not sure what he was thinking. He said, "That would be real nice, if you're up to it. We're going to see if we can arrange to meet with the judge at around 4:00. We could come over after that."

"And we'd like you, Mom and Dad, to meet us at the courthouse and stand up for us."

Edna and Robert were dumbstruck. "Really?" asked Robert. "Us? Your parents?"

"Yes," said Rose. "And that's really all we want to be there. We'd love to go over to John and Jackie's afterward. We could even stop by on our way and pick up something to bring for dinner."

"Don't be ridiculous, Rose! I'll fix us something nice."

"And I'll order a cake," offered Celeste.

Chapter 39

December 21-27
Apollo 8 becomes the first manned spacecraft to orbit the Moon and return safely to Earth.

Rose and Edna returned to Newport Fashion Island to finish their Christmas shopping, as Rose had been so busy with party preparations she hadn't had time to complete it. She bought gifts for Heidi, Chloe, Pamela, Lee, Nick, Gustavos, and the other managers of Alex's various enterprises. For the crews she bought baskets of smoked meats, fruits, and nuts that could be set out and enjoyed by all. She bought gifts for her brothers and their wives. She bought Charlie's girls a phonograph to share, along with ten popular 45s: *The Letter,* by the Boxtops; *Kind of a Drag,* by the Buckinghams; *Georgy Girl,* by the Seekers; *Pleasant Valley Sunday,* by the Monkees; *Ain't Nothining Like the Real Thing,* by

Marvin Gaye and Tammi Terrell; *Hey Jude,* by the Beatles; *Harper Valley PTA* by Jeannie C. Riley; *Scarborough Fair* by Simon and Garfunkel; *Sealed with a Kiss,* by Gary Lewis and the Playboys; and *Suzie Q, by* Creedence Clearwater Revival. She also bought each of them a new transistor radio. She bought a game of Twister that they could play together, thinking that it was something that kids their age wouldn't feel too grown up to play. She bought her parents a set of satin sheets, telling her mom not to look while she paid for them. When she and Alex had been at the Laguna Art Show, she purchased advance tickets for next year's Pageant of the Masters. This would be another gift for her parents. She picked up some socks for Alex and a couple of ties to match the shirts she had given him for his birthday just last month.

Chapter 40

December 23
North Korea releases the Pueblo crew but keeps the ship.

"The bastards!" Alex bellowed. "Kept those poor suckers for a full year, tormenting and torturing them. We oughta go over and bomb the hell out of them, just like we did in Japan."

"Alex, I hate to see you get so worked up about it."

"Dammit, Rose, everyone should be worked up about it! And don't think they're not tearing apart that ship. Pretty soon they'll be building their own spy ships just like it."

They were packing to spend a few days in Placentia, where the whole family would gather for Christmas. Rose had spent the past couple of days wrapping all of the gifts she bought. She set the gifts for all of the staff under the tree, and asked Chloe and Heidi to distribute them on the 24th.

She was glad Alex had calmed down before they got on the road. On the car radio, all the news was about the crew of the Pueblo, so she turned it to KRLA where they were playing a steady stream of Christmas music, rock and roll style. The Cadillac easily held their luggage and all the presents, and once again she envisioned how nice it would be to have a baby riding in the seat next to her as she drove around town doing her errands. They listened to the Elvis sing *Blue Christmas*, Brenda Lee's *Rockin' Around the Christmas Tree,* and the Beach Boys' *The Man with All the Toys*, before Alex said, "I'm lucky to have you." He reached over, took her hand, and added, "I'm the luckiest man in the world."

Rose lifted their enjoined hands and kissed the top of his. "And I'm the luckiest woman."

"A year ago I wouldn't have dreamed that I'd be so in love today, ready to get married and be a father."

"Me neither. Certainly never thought I'd be marrying the tightwad who made me buy a fake O'Keefe." They both laughed.

After a few minutes of silence, Alex said, "I hope it's a girl."

"Really? I would love that! But I thought you would want a boy."

"No, I want a girl. Of course, I'll be happy with whatever it is, but I want a girl. Charlie and Celeste's girls are so cute, and so sophisticated for their ages."

Rose chuckled. "Yes, they are. But there's no guarantee our girl will turn out like them."

"No. There's always the possibility that she could turn out like her mother!"

"Or her father!" Again they laughed.

"I hope she turns out to be just like you."

"And if it's a boy, I hope he turns out to be just like you."

As *Little Saint Nick* came on, Rose and Alex sang along with the Beach Boys. "Just a little bobsled, we call it Saint Nick. But she'll walk a toboggan with a four-speed stick. She's candy apple red with a ski for a wheel. And when Santa hits the gas, man, just watch her peel." Alex stepped on the gas of their own red sled, a Coupe de Ville, and they drove into their future.

Epilogue

Alexas

March, 2021

After having read my great-great-great grandmother's memoirs, and someone named Dede who apparently had been married to my dad's father before he married my dad's mother, I thought I should add a few sentences to the story before too much time goes by. It doesn't look like mother will ever sit down and do the job. Her mother, my grandmother, whom I was lucky to have in my life until I was in my twenties, penned a few pages at the end of her grandmother's memoir. I am now almost 54 years old and I guess it's up to me to continue the family story.

I was born in May, 1969, the only child of Alex and Rose (nee Lefebre) MacKenzie. I grew up in a huge house on a ranch in Rubidoux, just outside of Riverside, California. Our beautiful house, which had been built in the late 1800s by my father's father, was mostly surrounded by new housing developments. This was a business my father started after 10,000 acres of orange groves burned down the year before I was born. But we still had about a hundred acres of oranges and a cattle ranch, and my father was also into adopting wild mustangs and domesticating them for sale.

My father died in 1996 at age 76. My mother, who was 16 years younger than him, is still living. She never remarried. Today she is 85 and living in a retirement community in Laguna Woods, just up the hill from Laguna Beach. She's doing well.

She was somewhat of an artist, although she never sold anything. Oh, that's not true. There's a funny family story about how when she first met my father she bragged to him about how her painting had sold for some exorbitant amount, only to discover that he was the one who bought it! When I was little she used to teach art lessons at some kind of a halfway house. But when it closed its doors she didn't look for another opportunity. No, my mother was the quintessential stay-at-home mom. She was active in the PTA and often volunteered in my classroom, went on our field trips, and did all the typical things a school mom did. She was also involved with many of our family's charities. As a matter of fact, it was her idea to found the MacKenzie Family Foundation, which through its trust still funds a lot of charities today, mostly local. And throughout most of my life she was on the board of the MacKenzie Local History Museum, which is where she met my father. Another funny family story, which I won't go in to here.

My parents were so different from each other. My mother was artsy, fashionable, trendy, and open-minded. And beautiful. So beautiful! When she met my father she had been living in Laguna Beach and driving a Porsche. I sure wish I had that car now! But the year I was born she sold it, as they had already bought a

Cadillac by then, so I could ride safely in a car seat. Safely? What a joke! How did anyone in my generation survive infancy? Those car seats just had a canvas seat on a metal frame that hooked over the car's front seat, basically just so the child could get a better view out the windshield and not get fussy. No seatbelts. No safety even considered, as far as I can tell. Anyway, we got a new Cadillac every two years for as long as I can remember.

My father was much more serious, or as he would say, responsible. Oh, don't get me wrong, he could be fun and funny. But he had been in World War II and really was from a different generation. But they sure loved each other, that was obvious! And he was so handsome! Even I, his daughter, could see that! My friends all used to tell me how lucky I was to have such great parents. And I was! I knew it. I was probably the only teenager in the country who was proud to have my parents show up at my activities or chaperone a school dance. I was always proud of them. They were exceptionally attractive and talked to my friends easily, unlike so many of their own parents.

As I have said, I was an only child, but I was never lonely. I had a lot of people around me, and I knew they all loved me. Aunt Pamela and Uncle Lee, for instance. They lived in a beautiful custom-made home in town, but they both worked at the ranch so I saw them just about every day. He was my dad's general manager for years. She ran a flower business that was located on our ranch. My dad leased her 1000 acres and they were all planted in a beautiful array of flowers just about year-round. An old guest house on the property served as her office. She supplied standing orders of flowers to businesses and the old mansions in Riverside. She had two sons who we referred to as my cousins. Larry and Bob were teenagers when I was born, but we were always close. Bob had a great career a marine biologist. He was one of the first to raise concerns about toxic dumping off the coast. Larry went to law school to follow in his father's footsteps, but after a few years practicing law he quit and became a writer for *Surfer Magazine.*

I was also indulged by our housekeepers, Heidi and Chloe. They must have been young when I was born, although I remember them as being middle-age. They worked for us until I was out of college, then moved to Colorado to care for Heidi's mother. They were a lot of fun and doted on me.

I was also close to my cousins, my mother's brother's daughters. Like Aunt Pamela's sons, they were teenagers when I was born, so when I was a little girl they were my role models. They were always nice to me, never seeming to mind that I was a little pest, which I'm sure I was. I should add here that Carrie, the younger of the two, married Pamela's son Larry. They're both retired now. It's just as well for Larry, as the magazine published its final issue last year.

I got married when I was 23 and was married for 25 years before we got a divorce. By that time, our two children, Tom and Monica, were grown. I'd never say this in front of the kids, but my ex-husband is a jerk and always was. My mother has since told me that neither she nor my father liked him. Dad died two years after I was married, and I always thought maybe it was a blessing that he didn't live to see how unhappy I was for all those years.

Unlike my mom, I was a working mom. I started teaching when the kids were little. My Uncle John was a teacher, then a principal. My great-great-grandmother, Carolina, was a teacher, as was Dede (she of the original and voluminous journals.) I taught for ten years and then went into administration. I am currently the superintendent of a district in Orange County.

Both of my parents' ancestral homes are gone now. The house in Placentia where my mother grew up was razed after her parents died. The land and the remaining orchard was worth a fortune. Developers fought over it, and eventually a business center was built on the property. The house where I grew up was demolished last year. My mom stayed in it as long as she could, but eventually sold it and all the remaining ranch land around it. It was too old, she said, and too big to maintain. She said it was an albatross.

I am proud to be a fifth-generation Californian, Southern Californian in particular. My kids are sixth generation, and my grandkids, should I be lucky enough to have any, will be seventh. Our ancestors on both sides, both my maternal and my paternal, came to California to plant orange groves back in the years when oranges were being used to lure people to the growing state.

The house I live in now is in a beautiful area of Huntington Beach, near the harbor. Although large and beautiful, it looks pretty much like all the other new houses that have been built in the past decade. They look like they'd much rather be in Tuscany, but somehow mistakenly got erected in Southern California. I have a small yard in front and a small one in back. I have landscapers who come out once a week and maintain the shrubs and few flowers I've planted. But I've told them not to touch the orange tree. No, I'll take care of that myself.

When I tend to it, I can envision my ancestors. I can see them working the ground, laying irrigation lines, pruning the trees, and harvesting their bounty. My heritage comes to me from faraway places such as West Point, Tennessee, Peru, Paris, Guadalcanal, as well as places close to me, like Riverside and Placentia. I smell this heritage every time I breathe in the exquisite and seductive aroma of the orange blossoms. It will always be a part of me.

My descendants won't be able to smell our heritage because none of them will have had the privilege of growing up surrounded by orange groves. But maybe, years from now when they peel a naval orange or slice into a Valencia, and feel the citrus oil on the leathery skin, lick the sweet juice as it trickles onto their arm, or breath in the sweet aroma of the brightly colored pulp, they will feel a connection to the people who moved here 150 years ago and created the legacy that was to become ours.

Author's Notes

My great-great grandparents were early founders of
Placentia, California, where they planted orange groves
and prospered for many years. Carolina Borrameo
Polhemus was born in Peru, the daughter of Rosa Garay
and American Charles Polhemus. Carolina's
grandfather was the governor of Lima. Her mother died
the day Carolina was born, and her father brought her
back to San Francisco where she was raised. She
married John Tuffree who had fought for the South in
the Civil War and together they became well-respected
landowners in Southern California.   Currently in
Placentia, there is a street named Borameo and another
street named Tuffree. They intersect in a residential
community that has been built on the property where
the orange trees once grew.

The National Adopt-A-Horse and Burro Program was
actually initiated by the Bureau of Land Management in
1971. I took the liberty of assuming its founding prior to
1968.   The horses and burros available for adoption
come from overpopulated areas, where vegetation and
water can become scarce for the wild herds. To maintain
wild   horses   and   burros   in   good
condition, the BLM manages the population growth of
herds through   the   application   of   fertility
measures, periodic removals of excess animals and the
placement of those animals into private care.

Camille Beckman is a skin care product company based
in Eagle, Idaho. I have taken liberty to place her in the
setting of this book in 1968, although the company
wasn't actually founded until two decades later. Camille

is the founder, and her daughter Roshan is the vice president of the company. Their product lines contain only the highest quality glycerin, natural oils, flowers, and herbs. Please visit their website at www.camillebeckman.com to view her product lines and learn about her foundation that envisions a world "where women are empowered with knowledge, freedom and opportunity; where children and elders care for each other, and where all beings realize their complete connection to the Earth and all that is."

In 1968, possession of marijuana in California could result in up to a 10-year prison sentence. Selling was punishable by up to 15 years in prison. A third offense for sale or possession resulted in life imprisonment. In 1996 marijuana sales for medical use were legalized. In 2018 sales were expanded for recreational use. One can only wonder what Alex would have thought.

Acknowledgements

I am grateful to many people for their assistance in preparing this book for publication.

Thank you to Ashley Johnson, President and CEO of Visit Laguna Beach. Ashley generously allowed me to use portions of the history of this charming city that is posted on their website.

Thank you, too, to Camille Beckman. I live in Idaho, having moved here from Los Angeles after my retirement, and consider her a neighbor. She is a masterful creator of fragrances and natural skin care products, a savvy businesswoman, a generous benefactor, and a delightful person. I'm honored that she allowed me to use her name and products in this book.

I am indubitably grateful to Johanna Ellis, Board Member, Laguna Beach Historical Society for her unceasing search for information about the 1968 Pageant of the Masters. With the help of her friend Nelda Stone, at the Laguna Beach Library, she was able to locate a copy of the original printed program which listed the entire evening schedule of the masterpieces that were reproduced that year. What a find! And what a tremendous help!

In terms of domestic events, 1968 is considered to be the most tumultuous year of the 20th century in America. The *Smithsonian Magazine* granted me permission to use excerpts of the 1968 timeline they had published in a 50-year retrospective of that decade. See the front page of the book for the licensed permission.

One of the advantages of coming from a large extended family is that we have a variety of talents and experience. Below is a listing of my family members who contributed to this book.

My sister, Carolyn Bailey, "redecorated" the MacKenzie house. Carolyn is an expert on mid-century modern and leant her valuable expertise to the color scheme and furnishings used in this book.

Once again, my sister, Monica Fiello, leant her exquisite eye for grammar and English conventions to edit this book. Without her, the book would have unnecessary commas, mixed tense, and dangling participles. This book could not have been published without her expertise.

Another sister, Paula Hartgrove, is my marketing director. As a matter of fact, she recently used her experience in developing a marketing plan for the *Orange Trilogy* as the basis of her thesis. I'm not only grateful to her for her assistance, I'm proud of her!

Paula and my daughter, Theresa Voeltz, read the book and provided valuable input prior to publication.

My son, Robby Voeltz, a building contractor, answered my many questions about construction, particularly about the electricity that would be needed for the expansive projects undertaken in this story.

My great nephew, Nicholas Van Zee, a landscape designer, assisted me in designing the flower beds that Pamela created around the MacKenzie house.

Any similarities between the characters in this book and real people, except for those who are credited, are merely coincidental.

If you enjoyed *Orange Harvest*, but haven't yet read the first two books in the *Orange Trilogy*, turn the page for previews.

Page Break

Orange Champagne
first in the trilogy

Chapter 1

April, 1904

It was 10:10 when the train pulled in to the Riverside station. The ride from Los Angeles had taken just under four hours, including the transfer from Colton, but Dede was stiff and found it difficult to walk when she first stood up from the seat. She stepped off the train and noticed how little it had changed. When she had been here 15 years ago the Southern Pacific station had only one track, a platform, and a small ticket shed. Today there were two tracks to accommodate trains coming from north and south several times throughout the day and a small indoor waiting area for travelers awaiting their train or their transportation from the station to their final destination. Other than these two additions it was pretty much as she remembered it.

She worried that if she went inside she might miss her ride, so she seated herself on a wooden bench on the far side of the platform and waited for him. She smoothed the skirt of her two-piece dress, one of her favorites despite its simplicity. It was a pale green, tucked, linen, shirt-waist blouse, on which she had embroidered the collar and cuffs in a slightly darker green. She had made the circular skirt from the same green linen, so the appearance was that of a dress, rather than a skirt and blouse. It wasn't new, but it was comfortable and looked presentable. More than presentable, she thought.

Dede wasn't actually sure he would be there to get her. When she had first written to Mr. MacKenzie he responded that he was too busy and didn't have time to entertain a guest. She wrote back assuring him that she would only be visiting for one night. He didn't even bother to respond to that letter. But for some reason she believed he would come. *One night*, she thought, *then I'll go back home and it will all be over.* She pulled her small valise closer to her feet and looked around.

Cole had told her to write to Mr. MacKenzie if she needed help. He said Mr. MacKenzie would be kind and discreet. At the time she had been surprised to hear Cole mention his name; even more surprised to learn that he had remained in touch with him after all these years. Dede had only met Mr. MacKenzie once, those 15 years ago, and assumed that was the last Cole had seen him too. But Cole told her he had done some work with him throughout the years and they had become friends. He told her Mr. MacKenzie's address and telephone number were on his desk in his office. Funny, she thought, that Cole would include a telephone number. He never had a telephone installed in their own house. Never had electricity installed either, for that matter. Thinking of Cole and his avoidance of modern conveniences made her smile, briefly.

Dede thought back to that day 15 years ago. Mr. MacKenzie had worked with Cole to lay a rail track around the MacKenzie Ranch. For over a year Cole spent most of the week in Riverside, only coming back to Los Angeles to check in at his office and then spend a couple of nights at home.

Mr. MacKenzie had vast acres of orange groves. During the harvest, the fruit would be picked, placed in wagons, and driven to the city to be sorted. From there they would be hauled to Los Angeles, where they would be sold to buyers, boxed, labeled and shipped around the country. Mr. MacKenzie thought that by providing his own rail spur with his own locomotive and three goods wagons leased from Southern Pacific from his orchard to Riverside, then coupling his cars to the Southern Pacific trains going to Los Angeles, he could deliver more produce, faster and fresher, to his buyers. Cole, who was the Southern California director of the Southern Pacific, had explained to her that the proposal Mr. MacKenzie had brought to him indicated that within ten years his investment would pay off by tripling his income.

They and their two children had come down that day from Santa Monica by way of Los Angeles to Riverside for the grand celebration of the first privately owned railroad in Southern California. With Cole's influence, Mr. MacKenzie was able to rent two Pullman cars to transport his guests from the Riverside station to his property on his own new tracks. It had only taken about 20 minutes to get to his ranch. After unloading the guests at MacKenzie Ranch the private train circled around his property and once again intersected with the private tracks leading back to Riverside to pick up another shuttle of guests.

They passed an outcrop of a town. Cole told her it was part of a land grant awarded to Louis Rubidoux, an early settler in the area, and people called the town after the landowner.

When she and Cole, with Hanna and Jonathan in tow, arrived at the MacKenzie Ranch Dede thought she had never seen anything quite like it. This was the biggest log cabin she had ever seen. But to call it a log cabin was to do this house an injustice. This was a beautiful, elegant home, made of cedar logs. The entire west-facing front of it was glass. There was a porch that wrapped around the bottom level and another porch that wrapped around the second level. Wide steps led up to the porch and the front door.

Many of the guests were congregated on the lawn where the lunch would be served. An equal number had found their way into the house where Dede and Cole joined them. She was awed by the interior of the house. As she walked in to the main room, she saw a grand piano at the far end along the south wall. There was also a huge fireplace on the long wall. Three sitting areas offered room for guests to mingle for group conversations or isolated private discussions. Farther over, along the north wall but not separated by a physical divider, was a dining table that seated 12. Fresh flowers in overlarge vases were displayed throughout the room. As Cole was talking to two men and Dede was taking in the beauty and size of the house, Mr. MacKenzie called from the door to invite everyone outside where lunch was being served.

Outside Dede took in the aroma of the orange groves. She had become so accustomed to the smell of the ocean that she had forgotten the smell of agriculture. She stood for a moment to take deep breaths, enjoying the freshness of the perfume that was both sweet and pungent at the same time.

She soon became aware that Mr. MacKenzie's estate also included a cattle ranch which provided the steaks and ribs. Dede had never eaten ribs the way they were served here. She had always considered the rib bones just for use in soups or stews. But these ribs still had a lot of meat on them. A serving lady explained that they had been cooking slowly all night and day in a large pit dug out of the ground. A mixture of stewed tomatoes, molasses, and hot peppers had been spread on top of them while they cooked. People were picking them up and eating them with their fingers. Dede laughed at the incongruity of this beautiful estate and the primitiveness of these ribs. But she had to admit she had never tasted anything quite so savory. The feast also included chili, chicken, pork, and an array of vegetables, all cooked outside on a big grill. There were cakes, pies, cookies, tarts, and just about any other kind of dessert she could imagine. And of course there were oranges. Plenty of ripe, sweet, juicy oranges.

As people were finishing their feast the music began. Mr. MacKenzie played on his guitar and sang in a low, mellow voice. Another man played on another guitar, and a third man played on some drums. Some people got up and danced in between the long tables that had been set up for eating.

Cole took her hand and led her to a clearing behind the rows of tables and they joined other couples in a square dance. Then as a couple they did the two-step, Cole's favorite. Cole always liked to dance. He had told her once it reminded him of his past, before the war took everything from him, including his wife and small daughter. Every time Dede danced with him she sensed that he was in another place, dancing with someone else. He was happy when he was dancing.

There were many children running around the lawn, sometimes dancing with each other and sometimes dancing with the adults. Hanna and Jonathan each danced with Cole and Dede but they refused to dance with each other. After dancing, the two children ran off to play with other kids, darting and laughing and playing games. Dede remembered how carefree ever one was, how much fun everyone had.

At 3:00 that day Dede and Cole prepared to board the private train back to Riverside so they could catch the 4:10 train to Los Angeles. As Cole was rounding up the kids, Dede heard a male voice behind her say, "I haven't really had a chance to get to know you, Mrs. O'Brien." Dede turned and looked into what had to be the handsomest face she had ever seen. So far she had only seen Mr. MacKenzie from a distance, and although she noticed he was attractive, she had not realized how beautiful this man was. He was tall, over six feet. He was powerfully built, probably from working outside on the ranch, she figured. His skin was browned, which set off his very white teeth. They were further enhanced by a thick dark moustache. When he smiled she noticed deep dimples in his cheeks. He also had a cleft in his chin. He had thick, curly, dark hair that brushed below his collar. Immodestly, she noticed that same hair peeking out of his plaid shirt, of which the top two buttons were undone. But his most spellbinding feature was his eyes. He had large, green, wide-set eyes that actually twinkled. *Could that be true,* she wondered. *Do eyes really twinkle? These do,* she answered herself.

"If I may be so bold, Mrs. O'Brien, Cole is certainly a lucky man."

"Well, thank you Mr. MacKenzie. That is pretty bold, but I'll accept it as flattery. And I find it hard to believe that some beautiful young woman hasn't grabbed you up yet! I suspect you like your life just as it is."

"If I could find a woman like you, Mrs. O'Brien, I'd 'grab her up.' But I fear there's only one of you. And I understand you're as smart as you are beautiful."

"You flatter me again, Mr. MacKenzie. I think, I actually feel it, that one of these days you will fall in love deeply and live a beautiful, contented life. Maybe not right away, but one of these days."

"Dede? Are you coming?" called Cole from the step of the train.

"I have to go, Mr. MacKenzie. You have a beautiful home and your hospitality knows no limits. Thank you for inviting us. Good bye."

"Good bye, Mrs. O'Brien. I look forward to seeing you again."

Dede walked on to the train and wondered if she would ever see Mr. MacKenzie again. She hoped not.

Chapter 2

"Mrs. O'Brien?" Dede was startled out of her memories by a man walking toward her. "Are you Mrs. O'Brien?"

"Yes, I'm Mrs. O'Brien."

"I'm Edmond. Mr. Mac sent me to get you. He's out in the orchard today. Here, let me take your bag. Is this all you have, just this one bag?"

"Yes, Edmond. I'm only going to be staying the one night. I'll be going home in the morning."

Edmond led Dede to a touring car around the side of the station. He told her that "Mr. Mac" had five automobiles but sent this one because it had glass in front of the seat. "Mr. Mac thought you might want to be protected from the wind and dust," he informed her. Dede appreciated the nice gesture. The car had a back seat where her valise was deposited. Edmond said it would take about an hour to get to the MacKenzie Ranch.

Dede had ridden in automobiles before, but mostly she relied on the street trolleys. Cole had worked on the design of the trolley system that wound its way through Los Angeles and into the surrounding cities. He, himself, rode the trolley from their house in Santa Monica to the railroad office in downtown Los Angeles. Sometimes, if he stayed downtown late into the night and the trolley service was no longer running, he would take a trolley from the railroad yard and operate it himself to the end of Wilshire Blvd, where it turned into Nevada Avenue, and all the way to Ocean Boulevard. Their house was on Ocean just one block south from the Santa Monica terminal.

She asked Edmond if he worked for Mr. MacKenzie, which she knew was a silly question because it was obvious he did, but she was nervous and needed some talk to fill the silence. He told her he did, that he was Mr. Mac's driver and that he maintained the five automobiles. He added that Mr. Mac had built a large structure to house the automobiles and owned the tools and parts to maintain them. Obviously Edmond admired and respected Mr. Mac. She didn't think Cole would have entrusted a Colored man with such valuable machinery but tried to put the comparison out of her mind.

The car motored down a dirt road and through the orange groves. Dede remembered that palatable aroma from the last time she was here. It seemed as though there were many more acres planted with trees, and she supposed that was how he was able to triple his income, as Cole had said he would. Increasing the efficiency of the movement of produce had allowed him to increase his production. *Smart*, she thought.

As the house came into view, she was surprised to see that the acreage hadn't been the only thing that had increased in size. The house, which she remembered as being huge, now had two additional sides on it forming a U- shaped structure, although the corners were squared, not actually rounded like a U. The shape of it reminded her of the grand hotel she and Cole had stayed in when they visited Chicago.

Edmond drove the car up a macadam drive to a paved area and parked it in front of the doorway. He grabbed her valise and assisted her getting out and on to the flat ground. He walked her up the wide steps and onto the porch, where he opened the door and called out, "Mrs. Olsen! Mrs. Olsen, our guest has arrived."

A woman with gray hair piled up on her head and wearing a long gray dress with an apron tied at the waist appeared from a room beyond the dining area. Probably the kitchen, Dede thought. From the look of disdain on her face Dede wondered if Mr. MacKenzie had shared her letters with this woman. *No, he wouldn't have dared*! Mrs. Olsen continued to look at Dede, seemingly examining her from the top of her head to her shoes. "We're going to put her in the first room of the south wing," she said to Edmond without averting her eyes from Dede. "You'll find a washroom in there with clean linens. Edmond, please take Mrs. O'Brien to her room."

Relieved to be walking away from those glowering eyes, Dede followed Edmond up the stairs. The room was not large, and Dede suspected

Mr. MacKenzie had placed her in the smallest guest room in the house to discourage her from extending her stay beyond one night. *Nothing to worry about there, Mr. MacKenzie.*

She freshened up in the washroom, which was almost as large as the bedroom. It included a water closet and a bathtub, but for now she just washed her face and straightened her hair. She had only brought one other dress to wear for the train ride home tomorrow, so she didn't change her clothes. She finished unpacking her valise, setting her toiletries in the wash room and laying out her night clothes on the bed. She hung up the extra dress in the narrow wardrobe.

Dede had made both dresses and was pleased with the way they turned out. She sewed because she liked to, not because she had to out of financial concern. Goodness knows Cole had supported them more than amply. Her mother had taught her to sew when she was about eight years old, and they both discovered she had a real talent for it. Sewing comforted her. It reminded her of her mother, and she was usually proud of her creations. Satisfied that she was ready for her undertaking and taking a deep breath for confidence, she made her way back downstairs.

She found Mrs. Olsen in the kitchen. The kitchen was similar to her own, although much larger and much better stocked. There was an icebox larger than her own. A cast iron stove against the far wall had six burners on top and two ovens, whereas hers had two burners and one oven. Pots and pans in all sizes hung from a large rack above the counter. Two entire walls included counter space for the preparation of food and above and below the counters were cupboards. There was a large marble-topped table in the center of the kitchen where she could see the vegetables Mrs. Olsen was preparing. Sprigs of drying herbs hung from a line above the basin. A coffee grinder and other kitchen conveniences sat in the corner of one of the counters. The kitchen was warm, comfortable, apparently used often, and obviously the under the reign of Mrs. Olsen.

"Mrs. Olsen, do you know when Mr. MacKenzie might be returning to the house?"

"No, I don't. I'm his housekeeper, not his mother. I would never dream of asking him to share his schedule with me, and I suggest you don't either," was her curt reply.

"No, of course not. But I..." She was interrupted by footsteps on the porch and knocking on the front door. Mumbling something under her breath, Mrs. Olsen wiped her hands on her apron and went to the answer the door. Dede followed her.

Opening the front door, Mrs. Olsen said, "Well hello Miss Melody. And Miss Annabelle. Who is this young man you have with you today?" Dede noticed how welcoming Mrs. Olsen was to these three, certainly much different than she had been to herself.

The young woman whom Mrs. Olsen referred to as Miss Melody led her two friends inside the house, introducing the young man as her cousin, Lawrence Hastings, visiting from Indiana. Dede saw that Miss Melody was a pretty young woman with blond hair and fair skin. Her hair was pulled back off her face with a large ribbon. She had pretty blue eyes and a smile that showed her nice teeth but didn't transfer to any other features of her face. She was dressed in a lovely, pale yellow silk afternoon dress, appropriate for the time of year and her surroundings. Miss Annabelle was about the same age and equally well dressed. Mr. Hastings appeared to be about the same age and social status of the girls – twenty or maybe a little older and from wealthy families.

Miss Melody breezed into the room as though she owned it, and Dede had a sinking feeling that perhaps she and Mr. MacKenzie were... but no, this girl was way too young for him. Then again, she was very pretty, and she seemed to be very familiar in this house.

Miss Melody's eyes fell on Dede. "And who are you?" she asked with that same lovely smile that didn't reach up to her eyes.

"My name is Dede O'Brien," she replied with that same twinge of guilt every time she used Cole's name. "I'm a guest of Mr. MacKenzie. I'm just here for one night. I'll be leaving in the morning."

"I see. And how do you know Mac?"

Before Dede could formulate an answer she heard more footsteps on the porch. The door opened and in walked Mr. MacKenzie. He was dressed in a woolen shirt and Levi Strauss waist overalls, and judging from the lack of soil on his clothes he must not have been doing manual work out in the orchard. Miss Melody let out a squeal of delight and ran to him, placing her arm through his and reaching up to give him a kiss on the cheek. Dede's mouth dropped open but she closed it before she thought anyone noticed. Melody's friend and cousin laughed good-naturedly and Annabel quipped, "Oh look at the lovebirds." But Mr. MacKenzie wasn't looking at Miss Melody or Miss Annabel or Lawrence. He was looking at her.

Sweet Orange
second in the trilogy

Chapter 1

I always knew that the father who raised me wasn't my real father. He married my mother when she discovered she was with child by someone else. He was a wonderful man, very kindhearted and generous. So, when I was born in 1850, I was named Carolina de Silva.

Carlos de Silva owned a copper mine about 100 kilometers east of Lima and provided a beautiful life for my mother and me. We lived in a large villa, with servants waiting on our every need. Our three-storied house was painted a sandstone pink and covered with wisteria and bougainvillea. Dark green iron work surrounded a small balcony outside of every bedroom on the second and third floors. A large piazza greeted visitors and welcomed them into the courtyard, from which there were many entrances into the house. But the main entrance was just inside the courtyard, to the right. Large, intricately carved mahogany double doors opened onto a marble entryway, which housed valuable artwork of paintings, sculptures, and tapestries. As a child, my favorite was a standing full-piece suit of body armor, as my father told me that it had belonged to Don Quixote. And I believed him!

My mother was a grand woman who was highly-esteemed in our area and even as far away as Lima. No one knew the circumstances of her and my father's marriage, and the two of them didn't seem to care about it either. She was feted everywhere she went, to lunches, charity events, garden parties, and political fundraisers. Although young (she had borne me at just 16), Señora Rosa Borromeo de Silva was a *gran dama* of Peru.

And me? Well, I was spoiled rotten. I came by it naturally, as my mother had been a spoiled girl herself. Her father was a highly-regarded military general, and she had everything a child could possibly want. Perhaps that is why, when she wanted to give herself away at age 16, she did so. And look how that turned out? She went from being the daughter of a wealthy general to the wife of an even wealthier mine owner. But, like everyone else, I loved her. She doted on me and gave me whatever I wanted. I had the best tutors who taught me Latin, geography, literature, history, arithmetic, and beautiful penmanship. I had nannies who taught me the art of genteel behavior. They also taught me to stitch, and I was found to have a very good hand at embroidery. To this day, I love to relax with a pattern on which I can delight in forming running stitches, chain stitches, satin stitches, and my favorite, French knots.

We went to the local church, the Church of the Immaculate Conception. Like most of South America, Peru had been a Roman Catholic country ever since Francisco Pizarro conquered the Incas in the 16th century. With that came the period of *ecomienda*, the Spanish movement to encourage their citizens to emigrate to and colonize the continent, thereby bringing more Catholics to their New World. By the following century, when Diego de Torres Bollo and Antonio Vieira, Jesuits from Spain and Portugal, settled in Paraguay and Brazil, our religious affiliation was pretty much set in stone.

I always loved going to Mass. I loved putting on my mantilla and walking up the steps of the stone church, which was over 100 years old at the time. I loved the smell of the incense, the glow of the candles, the statues of our saints and the sad crucifix with Jesus hanging on the cross. But the statue I loved the best was of the Virgin Mother, for whom our church was named. Anyway, I loved going to church with my mother and father, the three of us always showing up in the best carriage, wearing the best clothes, and sitting in the most prestigious pew in the church. I only tell you about going to Mass because it is important to me that you know, despite the joys and challenges that would visit me throughout my life, I was and still am a devout Catholic. But, I was a sinner, as you shall see.

Footnote: I realized later in life that many people misunderstand the concept of the immaculate conception, which refers to Mary, herself, having been conceived free of original sin. Many people still get it confused with the Virgin Birth, which refers to Jesus's conception without a mortal male.

We were a good family, loving, happy, wealthy, generous, and devout. So you can imagine how surprised my mother was when I approached her with my plans.

"America? No, you're not going to America!" she responded.

"Yes, Mama. I'm seventeen and I can go if I want to."

"Why, Princess, why would you want to leave us? You have everything you could ever want right here! And you're too young to go off on your own!"

"You know why, Mama. And I'm older than you were when you married Papa!"

That evening, my life changed forever. My father disowned me, and my mother stood by his side. I knew they were hurt, and to protect themselves from being hurt further they cloaked themselves in anger. But I was determined. I was certain that I could write to them and make it all right.

Early the next morning, I packed two suitcases, which is as much as I thought I could handle, since I'd be traveling alone. My mother cried when she hugged and kissed me goodbye. My father had left early for his office at the mine. He had left me money, enough for the voyage and probably a few months when I got to where I was going. I did not know then that I would never see them again.

My real father was an American. He was the son of a business scion in northern California. His father's family had a long history in America; supposedly one of them had come over on the Mayflower. He had been sent to Lima for the family business. Just what that was I had no clue. According to my mother, he had been young, very handsome, and charming. When she told him she was with child, he returned home, never contacting her again.

I knew that he was from a town somewhere near San Francisco, in Northern California, called Palo Alto. My mother and I used to laugh about it. Why would anybody name a city high stick?

I hired a carriage to Lima. It took me two days to get there. Both my maternal and paternal grandparents lived there, but I couldn't bear to see them and tell them what I was doing. They would have been crushed, which I'm sure they were when they eventually discovered my desertion.

There happened to be a ship sailing to California that would leave in three days, so I got a hotel room and waited out the time. I was excited, sad, blissfully independent, and scared to death.

Chapter 2

May, 1867

I disembarked in San Francisco on May 2, 1867. The docks were noisy and smelly, and there were men and boys running every which way. The docks were crowded not only with people, but with rigging and other shipping equipment and crates and barrels of merchandise that had been unloaded from both the cargo and the passenger ships.

I had discovered during the journey that the Americans didn't speak any better Spanish than I spoke English, which was minimal. The little Portuguese I knew got me nowhere. But I did find a sailor who spoke Spanish and directed me through the docks and toward the city. I asked him if he knew a family named Pullham, but he just shook his head.

The ship had docked in the early evening, and it had taken a couple of hours for me to get my luggage and find my way out of the docks, so I was quite tired. And hungry. I found a carriage for hire and, in stilted but passable English, asked the liveryman to take me to the closest and nicest hotel. To my surprise, he said there weren't many nice hotels in San Francisco, that most of them had been built in haste to house the many gold diggers that had arrived in the last two decades. So I amended my standards and asked him to take me to a close, clean hotel where I also might be able to get a small meal. I looked out the window of the carriage onto dirty dusty streets and thought about the beautiful villa I had left behind.

I was shown to a small but cozy room on the second floor. The hotel matron brought me a dinner of poached pike, potatoes, green beans, and a tankard of ale. I had never tasted ale before, and didn't particularly like it, but I needed something to wash down the food. I ate, drank, and fell into bed. I began to cry, and soon I was crying uncontrollably, wondering what on earth possessed me to leave my mother and father and our beautiful villa. I cried because I had hurt them, the two people who had loved me and had given me everything I wanted. I cried myself to sleep.

In the morning I freshened up, put on a clean dress, checked out of the small hotel, and started out on my quest for my real father, in the city with the high stick. (I learned later that it was actually named after a redwood tree called El Palo Alto.) The carriage moved down a dusty road, but I had hired a surrey with a long-fringed top, so I didn't get too dirty. I told the driver to head for the high stick city, and that when we got there I would give him further directions. Of course, at that point I still had no idea what those directions would be.

When we got to the city, he reined the horse to a stop and asked me where to go. Not wanting to seem uninformed, I confidently told him to go to take me to the library. Once there, I marched up the steps as though

I knew what I was doing. Inside the one-room library, I spotted a woman who looked like she might know every important person in town. "Miss," I asked, "do you know the whereabouts of a man named Charles Pullham?" Anyway, that's what I meant, but judging from her face I apparently didn't get it right. I tried

in Spanish, "*Donde esta Señor Pullham?*" She furrowed her brow, then held up an index finger as if to communicate "one minute." She walked away from her desk and returned with a young Mexican woman who would translate for us. I told the translator to ask her if she knew where I could find a Mister Charles Pullham.

"She said she couldn't give you that information," she answered in Spanish.

"Why not? She can't, or she won't?"

More translating. "She said she won't give out someone's personal information, especially someone as important as Mr. Pullham." Hmmm, so he was important. I thought he might be.

I told the liveryman to take me to the newspaper office. As I was stepping down from the surrey, I noticed two young women who looked like they might speak Spanish. I told them I would pay them if they would come inside with me to translate, and they agreed. Once again, I found a woman who looked like she might know. But this time I tried another tactic.

"Ma'am, could you tell me the name of the Pullhams' business?"

"Which one? They own many businesses."

"Are they all located in town?"

"No, some of them are run from the east coast."

"Which is their largest business that is managed here?"

"Well, I'm not privy to their financial statements, but if I had to guess I'd say that would be Pullham Trust and Land Holdings."

"Pullham Trust and Land Holdings," I repeated. "Could you direct me to their offices?"

I was treated with respect by everyone I met, even the library lady who wasn't very helpful. I suspect that was because of my expensive clothing and the way my nannies had taught me to carry myself as an aristocrat, even though my family wasn't actually aristocracy. I, in turn, was polite and minded my manners, as my nannies would have had it.

I paid the translators, but by their happy expressions and multiple "*graciases*" I realized I didn't understand American currency. I had given them each a $5 bill, which was apparently way too much. I had the driver drive past the building, which was a large granite edifice, three stories tall. Etched into the granite above the doors, in large capital letters, it read PULLHAM TRUST AND LAND HOLDINGS. I was impressed. My father was as rich, if not richer, than Carlos de Silva.

A few blocks away, I found a boarding house. I rented a room, and once the driver delivered my suitcases to the second floor, I dismissed him. I put my belongings in the wardrobe and ventured outside to find something to eat. There was a small hotel across the street which offered lunch and dinner, so I went over there. While I was waiting for a portion of beef brisket with gravy, some kind of beans I had never heard of, a dandelion salad, and biscuits, I contemplated what my next step would be. When the waitress delivered my food, she asked if I would like a glass of wine. To my delight, it turned out to be a merlot from Chile! I savored the aroma, my thoughts returning to home and my parents. I quickly dismissed them before I started to cry right then and there and continued to strategize how I would introduce myself to my father.

The food was delicious. The beans turned out to be what they called pinto beans, slow cooked in molasses. They were served over cooked dandelions, which nicely complemented the fresh ones in the salad. I sipped the wine slowly and thought. By the time I had finished eating, I had decided to "wait and watch." I would walk down the street every day for a week, sit across from his office, and simply observe. I would familiarize myself with the people who went in and out of the building and try to determine which one was my father. Before I left the small restaurant in the hotel, I had the waitress help me to figure out the correct currency to pay for the food. She was very nice and showed me how to count out one dollar and one dime, for which I was very grateful. I realized then how much I had overpaid the translators! No wonder they were so happy! I also paid for the remainder of the wine bottle and took it back to the room with me.

My room was rather large, with a west-facing window which allowed for a lot of light. The bed, although not large, was soft and comfortable. The sheets were starched, and a lovely quilt was draped over them. Two fluffy pillows allowed me to sit up in bed and read, as I had brought several books with me from home. A wash basin and pitcher sat on top of a dresser with a crocheted doily on it. The water was refreshed twice a day by the home's housekeeper. Partitioned off by a Japanese screen, there was a commode in the corner, and it, too, was cleaned twice a day. There was a desk with a kerosene lamp on it, and a wooden chair to sit on while writing. An overstuffed upholstered chair sat in the corner next to a small round table on which sat a vase of fresh flowers. A coat rack had been provided for quick hang-ups in addition to the wardrobe, which was ample enough for the clothes I had brought with me. The entire room was tastefully decorated in a variety of blues, pinks, and greens. The walls were white, as were the backgrounds of the upholstered chair and the quilt. A picture of wildflowers hung on the wall, enhancing the other colors in the room. I was quite satisfied.

As I sat up in bed trying to concentrate on my book, I kept thinking about how far away from home I was, and what I was trying to do. Instead of crying, I thought about how much I had learned in the past few days. I had found my way to San Francisco, in California, in the United States of America! I was beginning to learn some more English. I understood that *biblioteca* was "library;" that *donde* was "where;" that *la cuchara* was "spoon" and *el cuchillo* was "knife." I knew how to recognize a dollar and a dime, and I was beginning to learn the value of American currency. Most of all, I had learned where my father worked, and soon I would meet him.

There was a mirror hanging on the wall above the desk. I took a good look at myself and contemplated what my father my think of me. I think I would be considered pretty my most standards. I had pretty skin, flawless and slightly olive toned, a nice reminder of my heritage. I had large brown eyes, slightly slanted, which gave me a rather exotic look. I wore my hair then, as I still do, in an uptwist. It was very long, almost to my waist, and I parted it in the middle before I twisted it up. I was accustomed to my nanny or one of the servants doing this for me, but the first morning I was alone I had to do it myself. My first attempts yielded a crooked twist, or too low of a twist, or strands of hair falling out of the twist. But practice makes perfect, and the more I did it the better I got.

I woke early the next morning and walked down the street to watch the building. There was no place to sit directly across from the business building, so I moved down a couple of buildings to sit on a bench in the shade. I thought this was better anyway, because they would have been suspicious had they seen me sitting there watching their building every day. That first day, I watched many men coming and going from the building, but none who would

have been the right age to be my father. Most of these men were older. Two of them had dark skin, probably from Mexico or South America. My mother told me that my father, although he had dark hair, was fair-skinned. Two women entered the building in the morning and didn't come out all day. I figured they must have been secretaries. A cleaning woman exited the building about 10:00.

At lunch time I went back to the hotel restaurant. This time they were serving roasted chicken with carrots and mashed potatoes. I decided not to have wine, as I thought that it would make me sleepy sitting on the bench. The same waitress served me. *"Como te llama?"* I asked.

"My name? My name is Virginia, but everyone calls me Ginny." *Mi* is my. *Llama* is name. I was learning fast. "My name soy Carolina," I replied.

"Soy?" she asked. Then, "Oh, you mean is!"

"Si, is." We both laughed. She reached out her arm and we shook hands. I liked her and thought we might become friends. I paid for the meal and walked back down the street to the bench.

Toward the end of the day, all the people I'd seen entering the building exited. I saw no one who looked like my father. I went back to my room and poured myself a glass of merlot and thought about it. Maybe he stayed home today, and he'll be in tomorrow. But what if he doesn't work in that building? What if, when I asked the librarian about Charles Pullham, she was talking about his father? Or grandfather? Maybe my father doesn't even live in this town. The thought was so disconcerting that I dismissed it. Of course he was here. His family was here. His business was here. Unless he went back east to work in one of their other businesses. That thought was equally disturbing, so I dismissed it too. I would return to the bench tomorrow and find him. With that plan determined, I lay down and fell asleep.

The next day was a repeat of the day before. I sat on the bench until I was ready to eat, didn't see anyone who resembled what I thought my father looked like, then went to my friend's restaurant. "Where *esta* Charles Pullham?" I asked her.

"Where is Charles Pullham? You know Charles Pullham?"

"Uh…no, not."

"Why are you asking about him? *Porque*?" Her Spanish was about as good as my English. But I couldn't tell her why. I liked her, but I really didn't know her well enough to share my personal life with her. "My mother know him," I answered her, not realizing that I had my tenses mixed up.

"Your mother? Where are you from?"

"Peru."

"Oh, of course. I've heard that Mr. Pullham went to South America. He went there on business. But that was years ago, before I was even born. So, your mother knows him?"

"Si. *Hace muchos años.* No…uh…"

"I got it. A long time ago. Do they still correspond?

"*No comprendo.*"

"Do they still write? *Escriba?*" She made a hand motion as though she were writing.

"Oh, write?   No,   no write. *Pero, mi madre* talk to me *acerca de* him."

"Ohhh," she replied. And she looked very interested.

"Where is Señor Pullham?" I persisted.

"I don't know. He's around somewhere, I suppose. I haven't seen him in a while." She spoke rapidly and I couldn't understand her, but by the way she shrugged her shoulders I got the meaning that she didn't know. She did say something about him being round, and I wondered if he was a portly man. That would be disappointing, as my mother had told me he was very handsome.

I finished the day on the bench and went back to my room discouraged.

I decided to write a letter to my parents, the parents who loved me and gave me everything I wanted. The parents who always kept me safe and put my needs ahead of their own. I had hurt them, deeply, and because of that they were
angry. But I needed to write to them.

Dearest Mama and Papa,

I've made it to San Francisco! The journey on the steamer was interesting, but uneventful. I felt sick most of the time, although we were always within sight of land. I spent my first night in San Francisco in a hotel, but now I'm in the city called Palo Alto (I know, high stick!) I'm staying in a nice boarding house here. My room is quite lovely. You need not worry about me, as I feel quite safe here. I've even met a friend. Well, kind of a friend. I'm learning to speak English from her.

Papa, thank you so much for the money you gave me. I'm spending it frugally and keeping it safe.

Mama and Papa, I am so sorry for hurting you. You have always been so good to me. I am so sorry, for I know how ungrateful I must seem, but I am not. I love you both more than anything in this world, and I do appreciate everything you've ever done for me. But, you must know, I have a curiosity about me that can only be satisfied in one way, and you know what that is. I have not met him yet, but I know where his office building is. I believe that he and his family are very well-respected in this area. I just want to meet him, to talk to him. I want him to recognize that I am his daughter. After that, maybe I can return home, and write to him. Maybe I can come here every few years and spend some time with him, and maybe he can come visit us sometimes. I think that would be wonderful, don't you have to admit?

Please Mama and Papa, don't be angry with me. I've cried and cried at the thought that you are angry at me, but mostly at the thought I have hurt you. Please write to me and tell me everything is alright now. And please tell my abuelas and abuelos I love them. And the same for all my tias and tios. I love all of you and miss you so much! When I come home we will all give each other lots of hugs.

I am writing the address of the boarding house at the bottom of this letter so you can write back. I'll hold my breath until I hear from you!

I love you so much. Thank you for not being angry at me anymore!

God Bless you both!

Love,

Your daughter, Carolina

Everything would be ok now. I felt so much better now that I had made up with my parents. With that I lay down and fell asleep.

www.ingramcontent.com/pod-product-compliance
Lightning Source LLC
Chambersburg PA
CBHW072234190626

46809CB00018B/2057